Marked by Lightning

Marked by Lightning

Molly Cobb

For Paul

&

For my family, thank you for your endless
support throughout this process.

Table of Contents

Chapter One

It was early. So early that the sun had only just begun to peek over the horizon. But it was already hot. What had been a humid, sticky night had turned into a wet, suffocating morning, and through this muggy air rolled fifteen military trucks whose brakes squealed as they pulled to a stop at the edge of the road. Feeling as though she was going to melt at any second, Becca Harraway peeled herself from the metal bench she sat on and jumped out of the back of one of the military trucks.

As her feet hit the ground, her dark eyes scanned the bustling movement of the Oakens train station. People were already swarming the small station building, vying for tickets. Clamoring over the noise of the people were tired conductors who were trying to create some order. To the left of the station building was a long train, the front of which was currently being loaded with boxes and barrels of cargo by tired looking military personnel.

A nudge on her shoulder pulled Becca's gaze away from the commotion. She turned to see

Neal Donahue, her regiment partner, whose eyes and hair were slightly darker than her own.

"Come on," Neal said. "We need to get out of the way so the others can come off the truck."

"Right." Becca nodded. She then slipped her gun over her shoulder and moved into line with Neal.

"Hurry up, soldiers," came the bark of Sergeant Nelson. "Train leaves in five, I need you all boarded and ready to go in two."

"Yes, sir," came the unanimous shout.

"Older regiments on first, younger ones will slip in the back."

As Sergeant Nelson's intense grey eyes swept the ranks of soldiers, Becca's followed. Four of their training camp's regiments were here today after having been informed last night that they were going to the city of Peumar to provide aid at the front. They had not been assigned tasks yet, but Becca was hoping they'd be helping with the fight. She wanted her chance at taking down Sarlic Lossi and his army. After everything Lossi and his army had done to the Edscaftian Nation and her personally, she wanted to do her part in combat.

"Soldiers, let's *move!*" Sergeant Nelson yelled.

Quickly, everyone shuffled into formation and marched toward the station. Their boots kicked up the dust on the road and sent small clouds hurtling off into the green fields surrounding them. As they moved, Becca noticed that the civilians waiting for the next train had turned to watch the regiments pass by. A feeling of pride stirred inside Becca as she caught their eyes. She was off to help end this war.

"On the train, let's go," the sergeant called again.

The clanking sounds of boots on metal filled the air as the soldiers jumped onto the train one by one and filed into the empty seats. Being in the youngest regiment, Becca and Neal were among the last to board. They slid into a bench only four rows from the back and waited quietly like the rest. Becca took her gun off her back and placed it on the ground before her; Neal did the same. Then they waited.

Sergeant Nelson walked slowly down the aisles of the train carts, counting as he went. Becca stared at him impatiently. She wanted to get moving now. The sergeant's stiff form marched and counted, and the soldiers avoided his eye contact. Becca bounced her leg agitatedly. A whistle blast filled the air, pulling her attention to the window across the aisle. Another train was pulling in, thick grey steam pluming out of its chimney. Becca watched as it eased to a stop and civilians mobbed its doors. Then she pulled her gaze back to Sergeant Nelson, who was getting close.

Leg still bouncing, she quickly scanned the heads of the other soldiers in her regiment—were they as excited as she was? Feeling a hand on her leg, Becca looked down; Neal was holding her still, his gaze focused on Sergeant Nelson. She took his hand off and sat straighter. Finally, Sergeant Nelson was in their cart, his eyes hopping from one head to the next and, as he reached Becca and Neal's row, his eyes met hers.

Suddenly nervous, Becca sucked in a sharp breath and forced herself to keep eye contact. Sergeant Nelson gave her a brief nod and continued counting. Becca slowly let the breath out, then sat back as he turned and made his way to the front of the passenger carts again. Another loud whistle blasted and a moment later their train began to move. As the train gathered speed, Becca quickly turned to the window and watched the green, hilly landscape flip by.

After the first half hour had passed, it became louder inside the carts. Soldiers began to loosen up and talk to one another, most speculating about what assignment they were going to be given, others just trying to distract themselves.

"Move over," came a voice from the seat in front of Becca and Neal. "You're squishing me."

"I'm squishing you?" replied another voice. "You're taking up half of the seat!"

Becca grinned at Neal, then leaned forward to talk to their two friends, whose blond heads turned in her direction.

"Aw, come on, you guys," Becca said. "You can't even make sitting in the same seat work?"

Nick Swartz and Lizzy Dowling glared back at Becca.

4

"You're lucky," Lizzy said. "You get Neal as a regiment partner. I got stuck with him."

"Hey!" Nick protested. "You're no treat either. Remember that one time when you—"

"Okay, no," Lizzy stopped him. "You bring that story up every time. You can't keep using it as your excuse to be annoying."

"You don't even know what story I was going to say," Nick said.

"We *all* know what story you were going to say," Becca interrupted. "And you only got a couple of bruises when you fell out of the rafters, so I don't know why you keep bringing it up."

"Thank you!" Lizzy said with a nod at Becca.

Becca smiled back and they both turned to Nick, who groaned and shifted in his seat to make more room for Lizzy.

"Happy?" he grumbled.

"Yes," Lizzy said.

A small chuckle came from behind Becca. She turned around to see Neal lean forward to join them.

"Don't worry, Nick," he said. "Becca comes with her own challenges too."

"Like what?" Becca demanded.

"Like the fact that you can't seem to sit still," Neal said with a pointed glance at her leg, which was bouncing again.

"So what? I'm just excited."

"Excited?" Neal asked skeptically.

"I am too," Lizzy interrupted. "We finally get to face off against Sarlic and his military. I mean, it's only what all of us have been dreaming of since forever."

"And we've been doing nothing but training for this for what, two years now?" Nick agreed.

"Well, *technically* we've only been in training for two years," Lizzy said. "But Becca, at least, has been preparing for this a lot longer."

"You're telling me you didn't dream of helping the war when you were little?" Becca asked.

"Of course I did. We all did!" Lizzy said. "But you took it to another level. I remember one time when we were kids, Becca led a charge against the chickens at the orphanage we were in."

The boys laughed.

"Okay, laugh if you want," Becca said. "But I won that fight. And do you know how hard it is to get in a fight with a bunch of angry chickens and not get cut to bits?"

"Yes, I do." Neal nodded, still chuckling. "And it must have been quite the sight."

"Well, you can't tell me that you guys haven't been dreaming of taking down Sarlic too? I mean, we're all here, aren't we?" Becca asked.

The others nodded.

"I'm glad the Edscaftian Council changed the law about new recruits a few years ago," Lizzy said. "Can you imagine if we still had to wait until we were sixteen before we could join training?"

"Yeah, we wouldn't have even begun until this year," Nick said.

"If I had to wait until sixteen," Becca said, "I would have just snuck in early."

"There's no way you would have passed as a sixteen year old," Neal said. "You would have been turned away faster than you could say the Edscaftian pledge."

Becca shot a glare at Neal, while Nick and Lizzy hid smirks.

"I could have!" Becca protested.

"Neal's right," came a voice behind Becca.

Becca turned to see Ruth Miller fixing her red hair up into a regulation bun.

"They turn kids away all the time for trying to sneak into military training," she continued.

Becca shifted in her seat to face Ruth. "Maybe, but *I* could have gotten away with it, right?"

Ruth shrugged and crossed her arms over the back of the seat. "I guess we'll never know," was all she said.

Becca slouched against the window.

"Anyway, why worry about it, Bec?" Neal asked. "We didn't have to sneak in, and now we're heading to a city at the front."

Becca's eyes lit up again. "Maybe we'll be the ones who finally help win this war!"

Neal and Ruth looked at Becca skeptically, but Nick and Lizzy nodded their agreement.

"I mean, the war has been dragging on for what, thirty-five years?" Lizzy said. "I don't see why not!"

"Exactly!" Becca agreed. "Maybe now that we're joining in the fight, we can start to really push back against Sarlic. We can get back at him properly!"

"What makes you think we'll be fighting?" Neal asked.

"Why wouldn't we?" Becca asked. "Why else would they be shipping us to the front today?"

"It could be anything," Ruth said. "There's more to the war than blasting apart Sarlic's military."

This time Becca looked skeptically at Ruth.

"Becca," Neal said. "Look at all the regiments on this train. Out of all of us, why would they pick ours to fight? We're the youngest ones here."

"Why do they have to choose?" Becca said. "What if they need all of us?"

"They could need all of us," Nick agreed. "The reports that have come from the front lately haven't sounded too good... that village that Sarlic burned down, and all those families that died in the fires..."

Lizzy nodded, and the three of them turned to Neal and Ruth again.

"Well, I guess they might need us in the fighting," Ruth said. "But I don't know, you guys..."

The argument went on for a while longer, but really, none of them had any idea what they were heading too today. So, eventually they slipped into silence and their own thoughts. Becca faced forward again and turned her eyes back to the window. Their train was passing a small village that sat next to the Valley River. Becca's gaze followed the river, which faded off to meet the shadow of a distant city. Becca assumed that it was Athlney, but as she had never actually been to any of the cities in the Edscaftian Nation, she really didn't know which it was.

The hours slipped by and still the train bustled on, its loud wheels pumping tirelessly against the tracks. Becca's impatience turned to boredom, and eventually she fell asleep. Her dreams floated in and out of various battles where she led their regiment past Sarlic's front lines and toward the man himself, taking their chance to defeat him once and for all. Just as her dream-self was running through a smoldering village, she felt a sharp elbow to the ribs and woke up with a start.

Becca lurched up and, rubbing her side, looked at Neal questioningly. He nodded toward the front of the train, where Sergeant Nelson was getting up from his seat. He slowly moved into the aisle and faced the soldiers. The few who were still whispering to each other fell into a sudden hush, and everyone looked at him expectantly.

"Alright, everyone," he shouted from the front of the train. "We've almost arrived at Peumar, and it is time to inform you of your assignments."

Becca straightened in her seat.

"Regiment 424," Sergeant Nelson continued as he scanned the largest and oldest group of soldiers. "You will be heading into this battle and joining up with Regiment 389. As I'm sure you know, things out there are tough. So, keep your wits about you and your guns up. Stick together and follow orders. You're ready. Don't let fear keep you back."

Sergeant Nelson raised his right hand and grabbed his left shoulder in a silent salute. The soldiers saluted back. Then, making his way down the aisle, he addressed the groups further back.

"Regiment 425, you will be heading over to weapons. There, Sergeant Williams will inform you of your duties. He has urgent projects for you to

handle. Do as he tells you, and do it quickly."
Again, Sergeant Nelson saluted, and the soldiers
saluted back. "Regiment 426, you will be heading
over to the information tent. There you will be
given instructions on messages that need to be
delivered. Sergeant Durrett will be there, he will
inform you of your duties." Another salute and
return salute. "Regiment 427."

Becca, Neal, and the rest of their regiment
sat up a little straighter.

"You will be helping with the wounded.
There are many soldiers suffering out there, and
they need to be brought back home. You will be
with me."

One last salute and one return, then
Sergeant Nelson turned and headed back toward
the front of the train.

Becca heard a few sighs of relief around her.
Wounded duty. She turned to Neal, who too looked
relieved.

"Wounded duty?" she whispered.

"Yeah, wounded duty," Neal said. "What's
wrong with that?"

"Nothing," she said. "It's just, we can do
more than move stretchers. We've been training,
Neal. We can fight!"

Neal shifted in his seat to face her. "Becca,
helping the wounded is an honor. You know what
they've given out there. Are you really complaining
about being assigned to help them?"

"No, but… We can *fight*, Neal. Wouldn't it be more helpful if we were out there with them?"

He stared at her for a second, then turned forward again, saying, "You know the answer to that, Bec."

Becca was ready to argue the point, but the sound of a loud blast stopped her short.

All eyes flew toward the windows on their left, straining to see what had happened. A dark cloud rose up in the distance, obscuring the already blurry outline of Peumar. The blast was followed by a clamor of rapid gunshots and distant rumbles.

Becca turned to Neal, whose face had gone very pale. They were at the front.

Chapter Two

As the train eased to a stop, Neal moved to pick up his gun, his throat feeling unusually dry. He heard steam hiss from the brakes as he and the other soldiers stood up and turned their attention toward Sergeant Nelson. The echoes of the surrounding battle sent chills up his spine. Silently, they all saluted the sergeant one last time. He responded in like, then led the way off the train.

They filed out in rows, each stepping down and taking in their surroundings. To the right they could see the blasts and flares of battle that had engulfed the nearby city. Dust and smoke floated over to them with screams and shouts riding on its coattails. The oldest regiment paused for a moment, then without looking back, took off in the direction of the military trucks standing by. The remaining regiments stood and watched. Once the older soldiers were all loaded up, the trucks took off and headed for the battle.

How many would make it back? Neal wondered.

As the last truck was enveloped in the smoke, they snapped back to attention and broke off into their regiments.

Neal stepped into line next to Becca. He watched as Sergeant Nelson walked over to Ruth and muttered something to her. Ruth's red head nodded, and then she headed back toward the train. The sergeant turned around, briefly scanned the regiments before him, and took off across the field. They followed close on his heels.

The sky overhead was a dark grey, made even bleaker by all the smoke and dust that permeated the air. Neal glanced around at the organized rush that surrounded them; fellow soldiers were doing their best to ignore the sounds of battle while they performed their duties. Step by step they trotted past different groups—some moving and loading weapons into vehicles, others yelling and running off to their stations, the sergeants' tent overflowing with papers and maps, the supply station swarming. The other regiments peeled off as they encountered their respective assignments. Finally, Regiment 427 arrived at the makeshift infirmary.

Without hesitation, they went straight into the tent and crowded behind Sergeant Nelson. A wave of pain ran over Neal at the sight before them. Rows and rows of wounded soldiers, some with lost limbs, others covered in dirt and blood from head to toe, many unconscious, and a few screaming out in pain as the doctors attempted to help them. As he looked, his head begin to spin. Images of his father arriving home from the front—bloody bandages covering his right arm and leg—flashed through his mind, but he set them aside and took a deep breath.

He looked closer at the wounded. Some looked familiar, but with so much grime smeared on their faces it was hard to tell. Neal glanced over at Becca, who stared around the tent with a look of shock on her face. They shared a grimace and waited while Sergeant Nelson headed over to the lead nurse and hurriedly talked to her.

Sergeant Nelson came back over. "Alright, listen up. These soldiers need to be taken back ASAP in order to get the care they need. This means we have to work efficiently and carefully. All of you pair up and begin carrying these soldiers over to the train. The first eight carts will be able to hold them properly. All the soldiers behind this pole here are ready to go. Get to it."

With that everyone paired off with their regiment partners and set to work. Neal and Becca made their way over to the nearest wounded soldier. Bending down, Neal gently took the man's hand and read his name tag.

"Hello, Gelman," he said. "We're here to take you back to the train. Is it okay if we move you?"

Gelman nodded. Neal signaled to Becca. Becca bent down as well, and the two of them picked up either end of the stretcher and made their way back to the entrance. Once out of the tent, they moved carefully. Neal led the way and focused on making this trip back across the field as smooth as he could. He called out to nearby soldiers to clear the way and wove around obstacles while doing his best not to jostle Gelman. It was a long trek, and Neal was relieved when he and Becca finally made it to the train.

"Bring him over here," a familiar voice called.

Neal looked up, not believing his ears. Before him stood Matt Carder, whose sandy blond hair stood out against the brown and grey surrounding them. Matt looked back at them, a huge smile lighting up his face.

"Matt!" Neal cried in surprise. "What are you doing here? I thought you had been sent to Statmore for some hands-on medic training?"

"Well, it looks like I'm coming back with you," Matt said. "They say I've gotten enough experience for now, and want me to learn more fighting tactics. Man, it's good to see you guys. Come this way, we can lay him down back here."

Neal and Becca followed Matt into the train. As soon as they stepped up into the cart, the sounds of battle faded a bit. Gelman sighed, and Neal glanced back at him as they shuffled through the cart. The overhead lights illuminated his injuries more than the weak sunlight had, and Neal felt a pang of sympathy for him. His face was smeared with his own blood, and he clutched the stub of his left hand with his one good one. It looked like he had also received crude stitches on his side, which was covered in a bandage, now stained a deep red.

"Here should be good," Matt said, pointing to a spot next to a soldier who had passed out.

They set him down carefully, and Gelman gave a soft groan.

"Thank you," he whispered.

Neal and Becca nodded, then looked up at Matt. Neal walked over and the two gave each other a quick hug and slap on the back, then Matt turned and embraced Becca too. Neal smiled, noting Matt's scruffy appearance.

As if reading his mind, Becca pulled out of the hug and gave Matt an appraising look.

"Nice beard," she said with a grin.

"Oh yeah," Matt said, running his hand over his chin. "Haven't had much time to shave out here... It's great to see you guys!"

"Yeah, you too man," Neal smiled back.

"So, you're helping organize everyone here, then heading back with us?" Becca asked.

"Yeah, Sergeant Nelson said they shouldn't feel that they are alone, so Ruth and I are making sure they are all alright."

Neal and Becca smiled. "Ruth's helping you out?"

Matt nodded, absentmindedly running his hand over his stubble again. "Yeah, it's definitely good to see her. She hasn't changed a bit, has she?"

Neal and Becca shook their heads, still smiling at him.

"Oh, shut up," he said.

The two of them laughed and glanced around at the few soldiers lying there.

"So far, so good," Neal said.

"Yeah, but you guys should really get moving, there are more soldiers coming," Matt said, pointing behind them.

Another stretcher was approaching, with Ruth leading the way. Trying to hide their smirks, Neal and Becca nodded at her as they made their way out and headed back to the infirmary.

As they hurried across the field, Neal glanced to the right at the distant fight. Soldiers were running in and out of each other's way while making room for the trucks and tanks. Their goal was to push Sarlic Lossi's military back and regain the city. The Edscaftians knew this terrain, and Neal hoped this advantage would help their military take back their land.

"Don't you wish you were out there?" Becca asked.

Neal looked down at her; she was staring at the fight as well. "Not really," he replied, focusing forward again.

"What? Don't you want to show those bastards what we can do?" she asked.

"Not right now."

"Come on, Neal."

"No, Becca! I don't want to be out there yet. We're not ready, we'd just be blown to bits."

"Are you kidding? We've been getting ready since the day we were born! How are we not ready by now?" Becca shouted over the blasts.

"There's more to fighting than knowing battle tactics, Bec," Neal said with a shake of his head. "We're not ready."

He heard her grunt in frustration as they neared the tent. They stepped to the side as another pair with a stretcher headed toward the train. Walking inside, they headed over to the next soldier. Neal knelt down again and asked the soldier if they could take him. He responded with a small nod, and they set off.

Again and again, Neal and Becca traveled between the infirmary and the train. Their arms and backs began to ache as they carried stretcher after stretcher over the rough, torn-up field. In the distance, the battle raged on, and it was all Neal and Becca could do to stay focused on their task.

"Okay, you two, this should be your last man, we've almost got them all," Sergeant Nelson said to them as they pushed aside the tall flaps of the tent once more and headed toward the back of the nearly empty space. They nodded and, reaching the side of another soldier, Neal knelt down.

"Hello Thompson, mind if we take you to the train?"

"Please," Thompson grunted.

Neal signaled to Becca, and the two bent down, picked Thompson up with more difficulty than before, and headed out of the tent one last time. Neal led the way again, setting off at a slow trot and struggling to avoid the now familiar holes in the ground. Sweat dripped heavily down his face. *He needs to get back*, Neal told himself. *Keep pushing.*

BANG!

An explosion went off nearby, encasing Neal and Becca in a cloud of rocks and dirt. Behind him, Becca gave a startled shout, and he felt the stretcher drop. Neal stumbled to a stop and looked back at Becca's blurry form. She had tripped and fallen to her knees, causing Thompson to nearly roll off the stretcher. The wounded man groaned, clutching his side.

"Becca! We need to be careful!" Neal shouted over the noise.

Becca nodded and looked over at the battle. Coughing, he followed her gaze. More shouts and blasts sounded, and the screaming grew louder. A siren wailed from somewhere ahead of them, then the sporadic gunfire that had been raging since their arrival increased into a steady tempest while the thundering of bazookas numbed Neal's ears.

The battle was getting closer.

Neal lurched back into motion. "Becca! Come on! We've got to move!" he shouted.

Becca turned back to him, her face covered in dirt, and he assumed his was as well. Thompson began coughing heavily, and Neal looked worriedly at him.

"Let's go!" he said.

Becca nodded and hurried to her feet, and they resumed their trot across the field, breathing heavily. As he squinted through the dust, Neal saw the other members of their regiment making their way toward the train while more and more soldiers ran in the direction of the fight. A weapons truck drove past. Another earsplitting explosion. He picked up the pace.

They were almost there. More rocks were blasted out of the ground and came flying at them. Neal tried to swerve out of the way, but some of the rocks struck Thompson, causing him to let out shrieks of pain. Neal looked back at him, then at Becca, who now had a deep cut on the side of her face. They needed to move faster.

Sweat sticking his uniform to his back, Neal took a deep breath and pounded forward. He needed to get Thompson to safety, but the struggle to keep the stretcher steady was getting harder. Thompson grunted with each shift.

Just a little farther.

More explosions sounded. The shouts were closer. Flashes and sparks now lit up the dust particles in the air; now left them dark. Neal and Becca ran hard, all their effort concentrating on getting back to the train.

BANG!

A lone missile hit a nearby tower, sending debris flying in every direction. Great chunks of wood and stone crashed around them, and the cries of the soldiers inside the tower flooded their ears. A large blur came falling out of the sky and landed right in front of them. Neal yelled, lurching to a stop. Behind him, Becca skidded, nearly falling on top of Thompson, who was now on the verge of passing out from the pain.

Neal coughed and squinted frantically through the thick air. Then the lump in front of them slowly stood up.

"Are you alright?" Neal called.

The soldier, who was caked in dirt, rubble, and blood, placed his hand on his head. "Just fine," he said.

"You're bleeding!" Becca shouted from behind Neal.

He glanced down. "Looks like it."

With that the soldier shifted his gun, gently shook his head, and sprinted off towards the fray. Neal and Becca watched him leave, then, as yet another explosion erupted, pushed on again. The thick air stuck in Neal's throat and the stretcher now felt like it weighed a thousand tons.

Come on, almost there.

As they ran on, Neal tried to see through the dust-filled air, but it was so impenetrable he couldn't find the train. Another truck passed in front of them, pulling the air behind it; for a brief moment, Neal could see through the smog and spotted the train. Veering slightly to the left, he hurried forward, squinting as he searched for the right cart to enter. To his relief, Matt appeared inside the doorway of the seventh cart and waved them over.

"Quick, over here!" Matt called.

Following the sound of his voice, Neal and Becca made a beeline for the train cart. The pounding of their feet was lost to the noise around them. When they arrived, Neal jumped into the cart, then turned to help Becca ease Thompson's stretcher upward. They then followed Matt farther inside, still panting, and laid Thompson down next to another groaning soldier.

"He's extremely pale," Matt said.

Neal looked down worriedly at Thompson, wiping sweat off his own forehead. "Yeah, well, it was a rough trip," he gasped.

Another blast sounded off in the distance. Neal looked up and watched as Becca walked over to the window.

"Are you guys done?" Matt asked.

"He was our last," Neal said, turning back to him.

"Good, I'm going to need your help. We need to make sure everyone is comfortable."

Neal nodded, then he and Matt turned to Becca, who was still gazing out of the train window.

"Becca?" Neal called.

Becca started and spun around. "What?" she said, confused.

"We need your help," Matt said.

"Right, right, sorry," she replied, heading over to them.

Matt handed them each a medicine pack and a large water bottle, then explained how much to give each soldier. He also handed them a roll of bandage, noting that some of their wounds might need rewrapping. Neal and Becca nodded. Then Neal headed for the back of the train cart, Becca went toward the middle, and Matt stayed in the front.

Neal knelt down and looked at the first soldier. His name tag, which said Blount, was still etched proudly into his uniform above his wrap of bandages. It looked like he was sleeping. Neal reached over and gently touched his shoulder. The man opened his eyes slowly and tried to focus on Neal.

"You're safe, you're on a train heading home now. Would you like some water and medicine?" Neal asked.

Blount continued to stare at him, blinking hard. "I'm going home?" he asked. Neal nodded reassuringly, and Blount's face relaxed. "Yeah, water," he grunted.

Neal unscrewed the bottle and poured some water into the metal lid. Placing his hand gently behind Blount's head, he raised it slightly. Next, he placed a pill on Blount's tongue and lifted the lid to his lips. Blount drank eagerly, then sighed as Neal gently placed his head back down. He closed his eyes again, breathing heavily.

"Would you like your bandages changed?" Neal asked.

"No, please don't," Blount whispered.

Neal nodded, gave Blount a gentle pat on the shoulder, and made his way to the next soldier. This one really was sleeping, and her leg was wrapped in a makeshift cast. Neal knelt down again and was just about to wake her up when another soldier walked into their cart. They all looked up. He was tall and covered in dirt and grime like the rest of them. His arm was in a sling, his leg was wrapped up tight, and he was leaning heavily on a scrap of metal working as a makeshift cane.

"Do you need something?" Matt asked.

"Sergeant Nelson just got on board with the last of us, we'll be heading off soon," the soldier said.

Neal glanced out of the nearest window. Things didn't look any better. The thick clouds of dust had covered everything, obstructing most of the field from his view, but from the muffled sounds forcing their way into the train cart, Neal knew it had to be bad out there. With a heavy heart he looked over at Becca, who was staring out of the window as well, but with a look of intense anger clouding her face.

"Have you got any spare pills? I haven't gotten any treatment yet. Well, besides this," said the soldier who had limped in, nodding at his leg and arm.

"Of course," Matt said, getting up and walking over to the soldier.

Another loud blast echoed outside, followed by more screams. Neal was worried about what was happening, but he knew there wasn't anything he could do to help those soldiers right now. He could help the wounded soldiers in this cart, however, and he was going to do so. Turning away from the window, he focused his attention on the sleeping soldier again. After that, he moved from one of the wounded to the next, helping in any way he could.

Before long the train began rumbling away from the battlefield and the three of them had taken care of everyone in their cart. Neal and Becca walked over to Matt and gave him their remaining supplies. Matt took them, but then pulled out a small spare cloth, poured some water on it, and handed it to Becca.

"You should wipe up that cut," he said. "I'm going to check on the other carts and see if they need anything."

"Thanks," Becca said, touching the large cut on her cheek. She looked at her fingers and saw they had come away free of blood.

"It's dried up," Neal said gently. "You'll have to scrub it."

Neal watched as she put the cloth up to her cheek and rubbed it. She then looked at him and raised her eyebrows in a silent question.

"Almost got it all," he smiled. "Keep rubbing."

Becca continued to rub her face. "Do you think they'll be okay?"

Neal's gaze lingered over the hurt and sleeping soldiers. "Yeah, Dr. Rosner will take care of them."

"No, not them," Becca said, walking to the end of the train cart and sitting down with her back against the wall. "They'll be fine. I mean everyone at the front. Do you think they'll be able to hold Sarlic's army off?"

"Oh." Neal walked over and sat next to her. "I hope so."

Becca grimaced in reply. Neal watched her as she leaned her head against the wall and closed her eyes. She seemed pretty agitated, and he didn't want to disturb her. So, the two of them sat in silence for a while. Then the door next to Becca opened and they looked up to see Matt come back in.

"Everyone is doing alright," he said. "Ruth's got everything else under control. She learns fast."

"Yeah, well, anything *you* tell her she'll remember," Becca said.

Matt's face turned pink. Neal grinned.

"Did you miss her?" Becca asked.

"I missed *all* of you," Matt replied, giving her an exasperated look.

Neal chuckled and Becca grinned. "We missed you too," she said.

Matt sat down next to Neal with a low grunt. "What have you guys been up to?" he asked.

"Training as usual," Neal said. "They make us run, shoot, practice formations... the same old deal. Although they've been having us do a lot more practical run-throughs than before."

Matt nodded. "Makes sense, you all have been training for a while. They'll want to be able to move everyone up soon."

Neal and Becca stared at Matt. "What?" Neal asked.

Matt scratched his cheek and yawned. "They'll want to send you up soon. Maybe not to the front yet, but they need people out there, it's getting rough."

Neal looked closer at Matt, and it suddenly struck him how exhausted Matt looked. "They kept you pretty busy up there, didn't they?" he asked.

"Yeah."

"It's that bad everywhere, isn't it?" Becca asked, nodding toward the window.

"Worse in a lot of places," Matt replied, looking very serious. "These guys have got it pretty lucky compared to some of the injuries I've seen. There are a lot who aren't going to recover. My guess is once most of this lot is good enough to fight, they'll be sent right back out."

Neal clenched his jaw. "We'd heard rumors that things had gotten worse," he muttered. "I was hoping it wasn't true."

Matt nodded. "We're all hoping that… So, how is everyone else?"

Neal couldn't repress a smile. "Good. Ruth missed you, obviously." He laughed when Matt glared at him. "And Lizzy and Nick are as loud and unpredictable as ever," he went on. "The other day they challenged some of the older soldiers to a relay race through the rec room, so that was interesting."

Matt laughed. "Did they lose?"

"Big time." Neal's smile faded. "Those guys just went into that battle today."

Matt's face fell too. "I'm sure they'll be okay," he said halfheartedly.

Neal looked at Matt, then at the wounded soldiers in their cart. "Yeah," he murmured.

"And how have you been?" Matt asked.

Neal turned back to see Matt scrutinizing him with concern. "I'm fine."

Matt raised his eyebrows.

"No, really, it's okay… It's been almost two years now, and time helps. Anyway, did you hear any interesting news at the front?"

"Yeah actually," Matt said with a yawn. "Lots of rumors get passed around, and I know we usually see the soldiers at their worst in the medic tents, but you still hear a lot."

"And?" Neal prodded.

"Well, the last regiment I was with kept talking about Sarlic's latest push," Matt continued. "I guess he's really been working on motivating the Lossians to join the fight. Our soldiers were saying the numbers they have been fighting against lately seem to have doubled."

"You're joking."

"It's bad," Matt sighed. "I don't know where he's getting all these people from, we hardly have enough to cover ranks. I mean, we all know the Council lowered the minimum age for recruitment to fourteen a few years ago, but we're still outnumbered… Did you hear about the village over in Sharnwick?"

"Yeah," Neal said. "All those people…"

"I heard they estimated about thirty children died in the fires. Sarlic just lit the whole town on fire and plowed through to the next one."

"Disgusting," Neal shook his head, thinking of his own family. "Have you heard anything about their weapons?" he asked next. "We've heard rumors that Sarlic has plans for making a new batch

30

of weapons. People are worried we won't be able to counter them."

"I heard that too," Matt said with a sigh. "I didn't see anything out of the ordinary when I was there, but that doesn't mean much."

A gentle bump on his shoulder made Neal look around. Becca had fallen asleep, and her head had slipped down next to his. He adjusted his position a bit so she could rest more comfortably, then turned back to Matt, who was grinning at him.

"Shut up," Neal said.

Matt laughed. "Guess you're not one to talk, huh?"

"It's not like that."

"Sure it's not." Matt slouched against the wall. "We should probably follow her lead though. It'll be a while before we get back."

"Yeah," Neal agreed.

The two of them fell into silence, each lost in their own thoughts until they drifted off.

Chapter Three

The day had long since turned to night when the train pulled back into the station with a slow trudge that all the soldiers could sympathize with. They all knew, however, that there was no break in sight. Sergeant Nelson ordered them to take the wounded soldiers out of the train and load them into the military trucks to be transported over to their base, Dune Hills.

With silent nods the soldiers paired up once more. It was slow work, as everyone was walking the same path at the same time and only five stretchers could fit in the back of each truck. Their already tired limbs worked numbly as they shuffled on and off the train carts and over to the trucks.

As Neal and Becca were loading a soldier name Rodriguez onto one of the trucks, a shout came from their left. They looked up at the noise.

"Donahue! Donahue, is that really you?" came the voice.

One of the wounded soldiers was staring over at Neal. The soldier's face was deathly pale, but lit up with a sort of feverish excitement.

"I can't believe it! How are you here?" yelled the soldier.

Everyone turned and stared at Neal, who in turn stared back at the soldier. It was clear to Becca that he did not recognize this man.

"I'm sorry," Neal said with a shake of his head. "I don't know you."

The soldier let out a laugh that sounded like it caused him a lot of pain. "Sure, you do. Of course, you do," he said quickly. "It's me, Ed Adams. Really, Finn—"

The blood drained from Neal's face.

"As far as jokes go, this is sad. I can't believe you're here! I thought that you... but you're here!" At that Ed Adams lapsed into muttering, the feverish look still on his face.

Becca stepped around Neal. "Get him out of here," she told the two soldiers holding his stretcher. "Move him."

"But we don't have a truck for him yet," said the boy whose name read Stevens.

"Just move him over there," Becca snapped, pointing across the group of soldiers. She glanced back at Neal, who seemed frozen in place staring at Adams with a look of horror. "Not here."

Stevens and the other soldier picked up Adams and went over to the far side of the clearing. Becca walked back over to Neal and gripped his shoulder bracingly. Neal didn't move but stared blankly after the man.

"Forget it," she said.

"But he called me Finn… he knew—"

"Forget it," Becca said with another squeeze of Neal's arm.

More trucks arrived, and everyone continued transferring the wounded soldiers. All the while Becca kept an eye on Neal, whose gaze was constantly drawn to Ed Adams. As the last stretchers were safely arranged on the trucks. Matt, Ruth, Lizzy, and Nick came to stand next to Neal and Becca and together they watched the trucks drive off.

The remaining soldiers in the clearing waited in silence for the trucks to return, the weight of the long day tugging at them. They sat on the ground and stared out into the silent night. Out here, away from the battle, things were very peaceful. Off in the distance were large hills separating them from one of the Great Rivers. The river stretched on for miles and eventually flowed into the Styrian Lake.

Somewhere beyond the railroad tracks a horse whinnied, and Becca knew the sound carried from one of the nearby villages. Back here, toward the edges of their lands, there were no cities. Most people still lived on farms or in small communities, content with their lives as they were. This was fortunate, because as the war raged on, the villagers and farmers had been able to keep their soldiers fed.

As they sat in this familiar spot, Becca could feel her mind resting. But she didn't let it wander. Instead, she watched Neal closely, knowing what was going on in his mind but unable to think of a thing to say to him. He was still very pale, and Becca knew it would be a while before he felt calm.

Someone gave a shout, and Becca tore her gaze away. The trucks' headlights could be seen in the distance, steadily making their way back. Everyone stood up, rubbing their tired, itchy eyes. Finally, the trucks pulled up and the drivers waved them in. With grunts of relief, the soldiers climbed in and settled onto the hard benches. When the last of the regiment had hopped in, the drivers gave the okay signal, then made their way back to Dune Hills.

The silent drive felt long, and Becca gazed out the back of the truck without seeing. It was dark, but she knew the surroundings. More hills spanned far out and past the horizon, then forests; and scattered in the shadows of the hills and forests were long plains dotted with more villages and farms. As she stared blankly, Becca fell into a stupor, almost falling asleep as the trucks rumbled on.

Eventually, the shadow of their camp rose up as their truck turned around a bend. Becca blinked hard and gazed at it tiredly. Dune Hills disappeared from view again when the trucks twisted down the road, but she and the others knew how close they were. As the trucks ran over a large bump, the soldiers reached down and grabbed their guns. Another bump confirmed they had passed the familiar potholes and were about to pull through the gates.

Becca traced the tall stone walls with her eyes as they rolled into the courtyard, then sat up straight. A moment later the trucks rolled to a stop. The soldiers jolted out of the trucks, quickly formed their lines, and faced the already waiting Sergeant Nelson. He greeted them with his usual bark, then ordered them to clean up, eat, and report for their nightly duties. They saluted their understanding, then filed across the courtyard, up the stairs, and into the main building.

Inside, they moved quickly through long, plain-walled hallways as familiar to them as the lands they grew up in. They were dotted with many doors that led off to classrooms, the mail room, offices, and bathrooms. The soldiers thudded their way up a stone staircase and down more long hallways. The second floor housed the library, the rec room, more classrooms, large empty rooms for practice drills, and the dorms. At the end of one hallway, the girls branched off to the right and the boys to the left.

Becca performed her duties without conscious thought. She filed over to her bunk, grabbed a clean uniform, and made her way to the showers. They had three minutes each to rinse off. She hurried to keep to the time, then shuffled off to get dressed. Lizzy and Ruth were right behind her.

She made a face at them. They grinned, then followed her back down the halls to the lower floor and into the dining hall. Usually, meals followed a strict order and set time, but tonight the girls grabbed what they could, threw themselves at a vacant table, and scarfed down their food. Then, with identical looks of exhaustion, they waved goodbye to each other and set off for their nightly duties.

Within a matter of minutes Becca was standing in the courtyard waiting for Neal. They were on the first shift of patrol tonight. Sighing, she sat down on an abandoned log and absentmindedly rubbed the palms of her now dirt-free hands.

There was no doubt in her mind Neal was still thinking about what that wounded soldier had said. He wouldn't be able to let that go. Sighing again, Becca shook her head slightly in a poor attempt to throw off her exhaustion. The door behind her opened, signaled by the flood of light that poured into the courtyard. She got up and walked over to Neal.

"Ready?" she asked.

Neal strapped his gun to his back. "Ready."

The two of them set off toward the gate. They were to take up watch on the northern side of the base, and they had to make the trek over there by foot. "I know you're all tired, but we should have the extra watch out tonight," Sergeant Nelson had told them.

Sergeant Nelson was always a bit more on edge when he came back from the front, and until today, Becca had never understood why. They arrived at the eastern gate and signaled to the guard. He nodded, then opened the gate. The large metal doors slid open silently, and Becca and Neal passed through, turned left, and strolled along the wall toward the hills.

The stillness of the night calmed Becca as they walked. Crickets were calling to one another and the occasional owl hooted off in the distance. The light from the moon and the stars lit their way, and Becca felt comforted by the glow. She and Neal padded along steadily, their feet crunching against the dry grass as they reached the foot of the largest hill. They paused and looked up to the top.

"How are you doing?" Becca asked with a glance at Neal.

"I'm fine."

Then he moved forward. She followed, knowing he wasn't fine.

As they worked their way up the incline, Neal scanned the surrounding area before meeting her eyes. "How are you?" he asked. "You seem a bit on edge."

"Yeah, well, guess I am a bit… I can still hear the bangs and the screams."

"Me too. Kind of turns off the appeal of fighting, doesn't it?"

"No," Becca said. "I still want to fight. Maybe now more than ever."

They arrived at the top of the hill and Neal turned to her, confused. "Are you kidding?"

"No, I'm not. What we saw today was horrible, I know. It's just, seeing what Sarlic's army does, knowing that they are right there and I can't go after them… it makes me so mad! I want to help stop him, Neal. I want to help end all this, and how can I when we're constantly being shuffled from one small job to the next? How are we supposed to end this war if they won't let us fight?"

Neal considered her for a moment but said nothing. He just nodded once, then turned and looked out over the land below them.

Becca watched him for a minute. She knew he felt the same, somewhere deep down. Maybe today had shaken him up, but he still wanted to fight, she was sure of it. She sighed, then began her watch.

From up here, everything looked so peaceful. The hill wasn't very large—it was really a smaller hill upon a larger one—but it afforded a pretty good view of the surrounding lands. Nearby were more hills and trees, but in the distance the land opened up again and spilled out toward the neighboring farms. The sight was familiar, and Becca was fond of it.

With a grunt, she turned around for a clear view of Dune Hills. The buildings of the camp were tall and strong, and they came together in a large U-shape. Incasing them was a thick metal wall that protected against any outside attack. The camp had been Becca's home for years now, and she knew every inch of it. She knew where to hide from bossy officers and which halls not to run in because of their slippery floors. She knew which doors led where, and all the spots you were very likely to run into Sergeant Nelson. She, like most of the others, had spent the last two years here and had fully soaked in the ways of their military. It was in her blood now, and she was determined to make a difference someday. Just like her parents had.

Becca's gaze wandered beyond the camp. Behind the far wall were the training fields. Years of practice had left the ground there hard and flat, besides the deep mud pits at their perimeter. Very little grass survived over there. Farther out was the area they used to drill battle tactics. Piles of rubble and broken buildings had accumulated there. Becca and the other soldiers had spent hours of training out there, and she knew, come tomorrow, they would be out there again.

Behind the training grounds was a thick forest. The forest spread all the way around the southern half of the camp. They often ran through this forest, struggling up hills and sprinting back down and dodging trees along the way. They never went beyond the forest, but they all knew what was on the other side. The ocean. Sometimes they got a glimpse of it as they ran through the trees. Becca loved the sight of it. She thought it looked so open and free. It was different and new, and when she wasn't having dreams about ambushing the Lossians, or leading their troop to victory, she dreamed of the blue water and the soothing sands of the beach.

Becca clicked her tongue absentmindedly and turned back again, keeping watch on the familiar fields around her.

For two hours, she stood silent with Neal, watching over the dark lands. No change, no movement, no noise. In reality, very little happened all the way out here; what they were really keeping their eyes peeled for were messengers. Neal eventually let out a small groan and sat down. Becca grinned at him.

"What?" he asked.

"Tired already, soldier?" she taunted.

"Yeah, we did a lot today," Neal said, smothering a yawn.

"We do a lot every day."

"Oh, shut up."

Becca chuckled. Neal lay back on the grass and looked up at the stars, and she saw his worried face relax. She turned back to their watch.

"Hey Becca?" Neal said.

"What's up?" she replied, still keeping an eye on the distance.

"That guy earlier, you know, the one who called me Finn?"

She looked down at Neal. He wasn't looking at her, he was still gazing at the stars, but now his voice was shaking slightly.

"Yeah," Becca said, trying to keep her voice conversational. "He said his name was Adams, right?"

"Ed Adams, yeah." He shifted his weight and sat up, staring straight out into the dark. "He and Finn were in the same regiment."

She watched him closely.

"I knew I recognized his name, it just took me a while to place it. Finn mentioned him a few times in his letters, along with some others in their regiment. He and Finn probably were sent to Maytown together."

"They must have been pretty close then," she said, sitting down next to him.

"Yeah, and now he's here." He turned to her. "Do you think—" He cleared his throat. "Well, do you think if he gets all sorted out, that they'd let me talk to him?"

Becca scanned Neal's face. She saw a small light of hope in his eyes and knew what he was thinking. "Yeah, I bet they would... but Neal, knowing how Finn died might not make things better."

Neal frowned. "You don't know that it won't."

Becca said nothing.

"It's just—" he continued, then broke off with a gasp.

Becca turned and followed his gaze.

In a flash, bright-colored lights had burst through the darkness and lit up the night. Becca gaped as the lights shot across the sky and erased the blackness surrounding them. The colors shifted from green, to blue, to purple, and back to green in a smooth, flowing stream. The lands beneath were illuminated, suddenly clear and exposed.

Becca staggered to her feet. "Whoa…"

Neal followed suit, blinking in confusion. "You see this too, right?"

"Yeah, I see it," Becca answered. "What is it?"

"No idea, but it's *amazing*…"

They stood still, dumbfounded, trying to take it all in. The beam stretched farther and farther across the sky with each second.

"It just keeps going," Becca muttered.

"What is it?" Now it was Neal who asked.

"I don't— Whoa!"

Far off, the light stream suddenly broke and a section sharply curved downward and struck the land like lightning. A resounding boom echoed after it which sent a deep, almost primal chill up Becca's spine. She glanced at Neal and saw his eyes wide with wonder. Seconds later it happened again, this time touching down closer. Becca stared in amazement, another chill grounding her in place.

"Bec," Neal said. "I think we should move. We're too exposed up on this hill."

She couldn't tear her eyes away.

Neal grabbed her arm. "Becca, we need to move."

Another light broke free, much closer this time. Becca saw it hit the ground.

"Becca, *come on*! We've got to move!"

The fear in Neal's voice snapped Becca out of her trancelike state. She shook her head to clear it. "You're right, you're right."

Neal tugged her after him and they began to run for lower ground. The next second, the lights right above them gave a shuddering quiver that Becca saw reflected in the shadows around her feet. She stopped and looked up. Everything seemed to freeze; she could hear the wind whispering past her ears and see the stars, now faded behind the lights. They seemed to be suspended, frozen in time. The lights grew brighter, and she thought she heard a shout. In slow motion, she watched the beam break and extend toward her like a reaching arm. Becca stretched her hand up and felt the beams warm glow touch it, then course through her body with such extraordinary force that she was thrown into the air. Then, black.

Chapter Four

Neal watched in horror as Becca's body flew through the air and tumbled limply to the ground. Then the lights above him gave a bright, searing flash, forcing him to cover his eyes. A second later, darkness had returned to the night, and, panicking now, he stumbled blindly down the side of the hill towards Becca.

"Becca!" he shouted as he spotted her limp form.

He fell on his knees next to her and rolled her onto her back. Frantically, he looked her over and leaned in close to her face. His heart stopped. She wasn't breathing.

He set to work, hurrying to resuscitate her. All the while he struggled to ignore the dull pounding in his head that grew louder every time he looked at her pale face. Hot tears clawed at his eyes, but he blinked them back and kept trying.

"Come on, Becca. Come on…" he muttered. "You've got to come back…"

Nothing was happening. Neal's hands shook violently, but he couldn't give up. He leaned in again, trying to push air back into her lungs. Still nothing was happening. Desperate now, he grabbed Becca by the shoulders and gave her a small shake.

"Come on!" he shouted. *"Wake up!"*

"Uhh," Becca finally gasped.

A huge rush of relief surged over Neal. He let her go and fell backward onto his heels, grasping his head in his hands.

"Oh, thank God," he muttered.

He watched her take in a few shallow breaths, tears finally escaping his eyes. Becca coughed weakly, still lying limp on the ground. Neal roughly wiped the tears away.

"Hang on, Bec," he said, gently touching her arm. Then he reached down and pulled out his radio. "Gate One?" he said into it. His voice sounded shaky, so he cleared his throat. "Gate One, are you there?"

"This is Gate One," came a staticky voice.

"This is Neal Donahue from the northern watch. We've got a wounded soldier down. She was struck by lightning. Requesting the doctor," he said, scanning the hills around them. Thankfully, things were still quiet.

"10-4, N-watch. We'll take care of it."

Neal put his radio back on his belt and returned his attention to Becca. She still wasn't moving. He gently took her wrist. There was a pulse, but it was very weak.

"Becca! Becca, can you hear me?"

Neal waited, but she did not respond. His head started to pound again and he was wracking his brain about what to do next when she groaned.

"Becca! Thank God. Can you hear me? Say something if you can hear me!"

Neal hovered over her, listening carefully. Slowly, she opened her eyes and looked up at him.

"Becca," he gave a weak smile. "Are you okay?"

She let out another groan and dragged a hand up to her eyes. Neal waited a moment, not sure what to do. Then she tried to push herself up, but it looked like she was having a hard time moving. Gently, Neal slid his hand behind her back and eased her into a sitting position. Still holding onto her, as she felt wobbly, he looked closely at her face. Something was off.

"Hey Bec, how are you feeling?" he said softly.

She reached out and grabbed the front of his uniform. He could tell she was trying to look at him, but she didn't seem to be able to see clearly. Suddenly, her face went even whiter and she twisted to the side, heaving up her insides.

Neal jumped out of the way, his hand still on her back. He stayed close enough to hold her hair out of the way. Shakily she wiped her mouth and looked back up at him. It seemed like she could see him now.

"What... what happened?" she croaked.

Neal gently held her shoulders and helped her to lean back against the hillside. "That weird lightning struck you," he said. "You flew about ten feet in the air and hit the ground pretty hard. I sent a message into camp, they should be sending someone here."

Becca looked away from his face and up at the sky. She stared at it intently and gently rubbed her hands together. He still wasn't sure that she was all here yet.

"How long was I out?" she asked.

"Not too long. But I'm glad you're awake... I was worried you wouldn't wake up."

Becca glanced at him sharply, then winced in pain and gripped her head. "Why?" she asked through clenched teeth.

Neal blinked. "Bec, you were struck by lightning, you—"

"Donahue! How is she?" a voice shouted at them from further down the hill.

Neal turned around and saw Sergeant Nelson and Dr. Rosner, a small, skinny man with little hair and round glasses, jogging toward them.

"She's up, sir!" he called, as he stood up to meet them.

"Up?" Dr. Rosner wheezed as he came closer. "What do you mean, up?"

Neal stepped aside and pointed to Becca, who was now sitting with her head in her hands. The doctor stopped.

"What? How?"

Becca looked up at the doctor's stunned face, then turned her gaze back to meet Neal's. He nodded at her and, as she put her head back down, turned and addressed the doctor.

"We were running when Becca stopped, then the lightning struck. She was hit over there and the lightning kind of… lit her up. It's hard to explain. Then, there was this bright flash and she was tossed through the air and landed over here. I ran to see if she was okay, but she didn't seem to be breathing, so—"

"You gave her CPR and called us, yes, yes." Dr. Rosner nodded. "But how is she awake? How is she not affected?"

"Not affected? Sir, she wasn't breathing!"

"Yes, but her clothes aren't scorched, she has no marks on her… Do your clothes feel like they are burning you, Harraway?"

"No, sir," Becca mumbled.

"This is not normal, and you shouldn't be conscious, let alone sitting up!"

"Sorry," she said, her head still between her hands.

49

Sergeant Nelson stepped forward. "So what are you trying to get at, Doctor?"

"I'm just, I'm just shocked, is all." Dr. Rosner scratched his head. "Here, let me take a closer look at you."

Pulling out equipment from his bag, Dr. Rosner knelt down and lifted up Becca's head. This motion seemed to cause her more pain and she winced, letting out another groan.

"Sorry, why don't you lie back down? Alright, I'm going to shine a bright light in your eyes, I apologize in advance…"

"Did you see anything else?" Sergeant Nelson said turning to Neal.

"No, sir. That was it."

Sergeant Nelson nodded and walked over to where Neal said Becca had been struck. He knelt down and traced the ground with his fingers. He grunted, then looked up at the cloudless sky.

"This lightning, where did you say it came from?"

"The lights, sir."

"Lights? What lights?"

"The bright-colored ones, sir, they uh, they filled up the whole sky. You… you didn't see them?"

Sergeant Nelson shot Neal a concerned look. "No." With that he turned away and moved along the side of the hill, inspecting as he went.

Confused, Neal watched him walk away, then turned back to Becca and the doctor. Surprisingly, she seemed fine. There were no scars or burns that showed where the lightning had struck and left her. There was no sign that she had been affected at all, besides the headache. Dr. Rosner declared that she was well enough to stand up and walk, but she should rest back at camp. Sergeant Nelson agreed and relieved both Neal and Becca of their watch. A minute later, two more soldiers arrived and took over.

Neal reached out to Becca, slung her arm over his shoulders, and wrapped his own arm around her waist to support her. He kept a firm but gentle hold on her as they made their way cautiously down the hill. The sergeant and the doctor took off to investigate more of the area.

Neal and Becca moved slowly, with frequent stops as Becca kept getting dizzy.

"I feel like someone's trying to rip my brain out of my skull," she muttered, her eyes tightly shut.

"Well, you're doing great," Neal said.

Becca made a noise somewhere between a grunt and a whimper.

"Come on," Neal said. "The sooner we get you in, the sooner you can rest."

They followed the path back to the main gate. When they arrived, Neal steadied Becca, looked up to the watchtower, and waved to the guard. A buzz came from within, signaling their clearance, and Neal placed his arm back around her to help her shuffle through the opening gate.

"You've got it, we're almost there," he whispered.

Becca let out a mumble of agreement and let him lead on. Neal glanced down at her feet, which were dragging heavily, and did a double take. The gravel around her boots was moving strangely. It seemed to be gliding away from her. Not in the way that the rocks bounced and skidded under his tread, but a smooth slide away from each impact of her foot.

Weird.

He looked up at Becca, but she didn't seem to notice anything. Slowly, they made their way into the building. They inched down hallways and past locked rooms. The stairs were a struggle; they staggered drunkenly up them, Neal doing his best to keep Becca moving. She tripped and almost took them down once, but Neal was able to hold on to the railing.

"Just hang in there, Bec," Neal grunted. "We can do this."

Finally, they made it to the top of the stairs. Neal sighed in relief, then pushed on, Becca getting slower with every step. He was just wondering if he was going to have to carry her when they made it to the dorm hall. They were trundling down the hall to the girl's bunks as Sergeant Nelson came up behind them.

"It's alright," Sergeant Nelson said to Ruth, who was keeping watch. "Let him bring her in, he'll leave right after."

Ruth stepped aside.

"Help him find her bunk, then meet me out here, I need to debrief you," Sergeant Nelson told her.

"Yes, sir," Ruth said, then turned to Neal. "This way."

She opened the dorm door and led the way into the large, dark room. Sounds of the sleeping soldiers—occasional grunts and creaks of mattresses—filled the air. Following Ruth as best as he could down the aisles of neatly organized bunks, Neal practically carried Becca through row after row. They moved quietly, trying hard not to wake the others. Finally, they arrived at the seventh row and Ruth pointed to the lower bunk.

"Oh, good," Neal sighed.

Ruth helped him lay Becca down on her bunk, then took her boots off. Neal stretched his arms and rubbed his shoulders. For a moment they both watched Becca, who had already fallen asleep.

"What happened to her?" Ruth asked.

"She was struck by lightning."

Ruth's eyes got wide. "What?" she hissed.

Neal tiredly ruffled his hair. "Yeah, it's a lot to explain, but I'm sure it's what Sarge is going to debrief you on. I'll tell you the rest tomorrow."

"Right, sorry, you must be tired."

Neal smiled and patted her gently on the arm. "No more tired than you."

With that the two crept back out.

"Sir," Neal saluted.

"Donahue," Sergeant Nelson saluted back.

Now excused, Neal turned down the hall and headed for the boys' dorm. He rubbed his eyes, feeling the weight of the day more than ever. All days were hard here at training camp, but today had been especially so. He waved tiredly at Nick, who was on duty tonight, and entered the dorm. Shuffling through the aisles, he made his way to his own bed this time. He didn't bother changing. Instead, he kicked off his shoes, threw himself face down on the bed, and fell asleep almost the moment his head hit the pillow, the image of the lightning striking Becca still clear in his mind.

Chapter Five

The food tray hit the table with a loud thud as Neal plopped down between Matt and Becca with an exhausted grunt. Becca winced and waved her hand at him.

"Oh, sorry!" he whispered, looking closely at her. "How are you feeling?"

"She threw up this morning," said Lizzy, who was sitting across from them alongside Ruth and Nick.

"Really?" he asked.

"Yeah," Ruth said. "It sounded bad."

"I'm fine!" Becca hissed.

"You should be resting!" Matt said. "Really, you should be in a hospital bed. Anyone who gets struck by lightning needs time to heal, especially when it's weird lightning."

Becca looked over at Matt, her eyes bloodshot. "You're joking, right? It's not like I got shot. And Dr. Rosner said I was fine. Plus, that whole building is full of wounded soldiers, the last thing they need is a soldier who claims to have a bad headache. Dr. Rosner shouldn't have even come to see me last night."

"Shut up, Bec," Neal said. "You stopped breathing."

"And you resuscitated me," she said with a grateful wave. "So, the doc didn't have anything to do."

Neal shook his head and looked exasperatedly at Nick and Matt, who grinned back.

"Did you guys hear anything else?" Neal asked.

"No," Nick said. "There are a lot of rumors going around about the lights, but as far as we know, we're the only ones who know about what happened to Becca last night. Besides Dave and Lacy, and that's only because they took over your shift."

"So, Sarge swore you all to secrecy?" Becca said, picking up a piece of toast.

"Kind of," Ruth answered.

"Why?"

"He said something about new enemy tactics," Nick shrugged.

"Enemy tactics?" Becca asked. "It was the lights."

"Yeah, well, he didn't see any lights," Neal said.

Becca looked sharply at him, then let out a small groan and put a palm to her temple. "What? How did he not see them?"

"Well, if he was inside, he could have missed them," Lizzy answered. "I mean, *we* didn't see anything. But I heard that some of the others did. They said they've never seen anything like them before."

Nick leaned in toward the center of the table. "I heard Private Roland saying he thinks it might've come from Sarlic Lossi," he whispered. "But when Captain Stephenson walked by, he ordered them to stop talking about it."

"Why?" Neal asked.

"I don't think the sergeants want us talking about the lights," Ruth said. "I mean, look around."

The table turned their heads to scan the room. There were whispers amidst the usual chatter, and many of the other soldiers were looking around as anxiously as Neal and his group were. Neal turned his focus to the sergeants' table, where Sergeant Nelson himself was whispering quickly to his peers. He looked serious, and tired. Neal wondered if he had gotten any sleep last night.

"Why don't they want us talking about it?" he asked, turning back to the group.

They shrugged and shook their heads. Becca gave a low grunt and dropped her toast. Neal looked at her carefully as Nick took a loud gulp of his orange juice.

"Well, whatever the reason, it sounds like we'll be training hard today," Nick said as he placed his empty cup down. "And I don't want to give them a reason to be angry with us if they're going to be drilling us all day."

Neal nodded, and the group dropped the topic and focused on breakfast. They only had a little bit of time left before they would be dismissed from the dining hall. All but Becca scarfed down the rest of their food, finishing just in time. When Sergeant Nelson stood up, everyone stopped eating and followed suit. They all stood at attention as he left the dining hall. Once he was gone, they scooped up their trays and headed to the washing station to drop them off. Neal walked behind Becca, keeping a close eye on her. All the noise really seemed to be bugging her, although she was doing her best to hide it.

Following everyone else, they shuffled down the line and dropped off their trays, but as Becca set hers down Neal saw the leftover food on the tray below it scatter, flying across the counter. Becca was already walking away. Confused and tired, Neal figured he must have imagined it and said nothing.

Still in orderly queue, they headed down the long hallways to the gym. This is where their morning training often started; it wouldn't be long before they were out on the grounds doing tactics and drills. Everyone marched into line, then stood at attention as the drill sergeants filed into the room. They stood stock still as inspection commenced, waiting for their orders. The gym doors burst open, the echo traveling throughout the silent room, and to everyone's surprise, Sergeant Nelson strode in. Anticipating an announcement, all eyes watched as he passed to the center of the room.

"Soldiers. I hope you enjoyed your easy morning. Tomorrow you will not be so lucky. We need to train harder, as this war will soon be yours to fight. Something has come to my attention that leads me to believe that the enemy is making another attempt to turn the war in their favor. So, we'll be kicking training up a notch." He turned toward the drill sergeants. "You know what to do."

With that the drill sergeants turned back towards their regiments and shouted at them to run a lap around the gym, then proceed out to the grounds. Moving past all the commotion, Sergeant Nelson walked over to the drill sergeant of Becca and Neal's regiment and whispered something in his ear before heading for the door.

"Donahue, Harraway. Front and center," yelled their drill sergeant.

Neal and Becca shared a nervous glance as they stepped forward, trying to ignore the looks they were getting.

"Sergeant Nelson wants to see you in his office immediately. You will rejoin training when you are done."

"Yes, sir," they saluted. They then turned and made their way out of the gymnasium with the sounds of running feet and shouting drill sergeants echoing after them.

As the door closed behind them Becca stopped and clutched her head in both hands. Alarmed, Neal reached out and steadied her.

"Are you okay?"

Becca slightly shook her head. Concerned and a little worried, Neal moved closer.

"Are you sure you can make it to Sergeant Nelson's office?"

Becca nodded slowly, her eyes shut tight, but gripped Neal's arm. He gently placed his hand on top of hers and led her forward. They made their way gingerly through the silent halls until they arrived at Sergeant Nelson's office. Neal stepped forward and knocked twice.

"Enter," came the sergeant's voice.

Neal glanced once more at Becca. She took a deep breath and stood up tall—trying to conceal her pain, he knew. Reaching out, he turned the handle and opened the door. They entered the room with a salute and stood at attention, their hands at their sides.

The room was plain and simple. A sturdy brown desk stood in the center, with two wooden chairs in front of it. To the left was a metal filing cabinet, and to the right, a table full of papers, maps, and a phone. A dying plant stood in the corner nearest the door. The sergeant's desk was currently buried under open books, papers, and pens.

Sergeant Nelson was sitting at the desk, scribbling on one of the loose papers. "At ease," he said with a quick glance at them.

Neal and Becca spread their feet and placed their hands behind their backs. Becca swayed slightly in Neal's peripheral vision.

"I believe the two of you know why I called you here. I am concerned about the events of last night, and I'd like to go further into the details of what happened. I suspect the enemy might be behind it."

Sergeant Nelson laid down his pen and looked up, studying the two of them.

"What would you like to know, sir?" Neal said.

"I need the details of the moments leading up to the lightning strike," he said. "Every detail. Help us figure out what this was."

Neal nodded. He could feel Becca shaking next to him as she too gave a small nod, but he refrained from glancing at her.

"All was still, sir," he said. "There was no movement on the grounds, and nothing to suggest that a storm was coming. The skies were clear, sir. Then, these lights came from behind us and lit up the sky, moving forward."

"From behind you? You mean from the south?" Sergeant Nelson asked.

"Yes, sir, and—" Neal stopped short at a low groan from Becca and moved just in time to catch her as she fell forward.

Sergeant Nelson leapt up and helped him lower her to the ground. Neal stepped back as the sergeant checked her pulse and breath. "She's breathing," he said. "Just fainted. I'll call the doctor."

With that Sergeant Nelson stood up and moved toward his phone. He dialed up the doctor's section number and requested his immediate presence. He then quickly left the room, mumbling something about water.

Neal stayed with Becca and gently raised her head, placing it on his lap to keep it elevated. Her breathing was shallow, which seemed worrisome. Suddenly her right hand twitched, and as it did a pen on the edge of the desk jumped to the ground. Neal blinked, unsure of what he had just seen. Her hand twitched again and the pen lifted ever so slightly off the ground and spun in a small circle before falling. Neal stared, sure that this time he wasn't imagining things.

Sergeant Nelson came back into the room and knelt down. "Tilt her head back a bit," he told Neal.

Neal did so, and Sergeant Nelson poured some water into her mouth. Then, dipping his fingers into the cup, he dabbed some water on her wrists. She gave no response.

"Sergeant Nelson," came Dr. Rosner's voice from behind them. "What is wrong, sir?"

"Doctor, good. Harraway has fainted again," Sergeant Nelson said, standing up to get out of the way.

Dr. Rosner knelt down in his place and checked Becca himself. After a minute he grunted and looked up at Neal. "Can you carry her?" he asked.

"Yes, sir," Neal answered.

"Good. Pick her up and bring her to the hospital. I'll take a closer look at her there."

Dr. Rosner stood up and whispered quickly to Sergeant Nelson, who nodded, and they both left the room. Neal shifted to Becca's side and scooped her up. Adjusting his grip to rest her head on his shoulder, he edged slowly out of the office and down the hall, following Sergeant Nelson and Dr. Rosner.

The group wove their way through the halls at a fast clip. Neal did his best to keep up, but struggled a bit under Becca's weight. They passed a few captains who were making their way outside. The captains moved out of the way, sending confused and concerned frowns after them.

They continued down the hall, finally arriving at the camp hospital. Sergeant Nelson and Dr. Rosner held open the doors as Neal passed through with Becca. The great room was full of single beds, most of which were occupied by the wounded they had brought back yesterday. Already, these soldiers looked a lot better. They were cleaned up, in fresh clothes, and no longer groaning in pain. Those with lesser injuries were up and helping the nurses with the more seriously injured. The curtains around some of the beds were closed, but most were open, so many eyes looked on curiously as Neal made his way to the nearest empty bed and laid Becca down on it.

Dr. Rosner came up behind him, waving to a nurse to come help. As she bustled over, he pushed Neal back and drew the curtains around Becca's bed. Neal stepped next to Sergeant Nelson and awaited orders, but Sergeant Nelson stood still, waiting.

The soldiers that could move well enough saluted Sergeant Nelson, having noticed his entrance. Sergeant Nelson acknowledged this effort and saluted them back, then gestured for them to sit and rest.

Chewing his lip nervously, Neal looked around. The ward was clean, and it was clear that they took good care of it. Beds were lined up against opposite walls, both featuring rows of tall, sparkling windows. Ample sunlight was supposed to help the patients heal. Matt had told Neal that it helped keep the wounded from getting too depressed.

Small wooden tables stood in between every bed. Each table had a glass of water on it, and many held various other things as well, from tissues, to books, to flowers. At the far end of the room were doors to two smaller rooms. Neal knew these were Dr. Rosner's and the nurses' offices.

As Neal stood there waiting, he scanned the beds for Ed Adams, with the hope that maybe he could come back later and talk to him. He skimmed the room twice, but there was no sign of Adams.

He must be behind one of the curtains, Neal thought.

A cough came from behind Becca's curtains, bringing Neal's attention back to her. A frustrated sigh and a loud groan told Neal that she was up. He let out a breath of air, stealing a glance at Sergeant Nelson, who looked down at him. Neal nodded awkwardly and looked away.

Dr. Rosner's voice followed a murmur from the nurse, but Neal couldn't quite make out what he said. The nurse hurried out of the curtained space and to her office. While she was gone, hushed voices came floating over to them. Clearly, Becca wasn't happy. The nurse came back and slid between the curtains again, and seconds later the doctor hurried out and made his way over to Sergeant Nelson.

"Okay, Sergeant. She is awake but her head is still reacting to what happened last night, so she'll need to stay here until we can figure out what is going on. Hopefully, it won't take us very long and she can go back to training soon. Until then, she just needs to rest."

"Thank you, Doctor," Sergeant Nelson replied. "Is there anything else?"

"Not at the moment, no."

"Keep me informed."

"Yes, sir."

"Well then, you should get back to drills," Sergeant Nelson said, turning to Neal.

"Yes, sir," Neal said. With a salute, he turned and headed back out of the hospital, thoughts filled with Becca and the floating pen.

***

"How was she when you left her?" Lizzy whispered to Neal as they waited in line to crawl through the mud under a very low bridge.

"Fine, I guess." He shrugged. "Dr. Rosner said she needs to rest for now. They don't know how long she'll be in there."

"She's not going to like that."

Neal smiled. "Not a bit."

He was next. He squatted down, and as enough space cleared, he lowered himself onto his belly and crawled through the mud. Neal had never understood the purpose of this exercise but figured that the drill sergeants had a good reason for making them do it over and over again.

Lizzy filed in after Neal, and Matt after her. Each slopping through the mud toward the grinning drill sergeants waiting on the other side. Every regiment was being worked to the bone. If Sergeant Nelson was tense, everyone was, and it always showed when it came to their training.

It was made clear that no one could be good enough at drills today. They climbed clumsily, reacted poorly, and ran sluggishly. The drill sergeants didn't ease up as the sun crept to the top of the sky and westward. They were given no lunch break. Instead, they went on a ten-mile run with guns on their backs, up through the hills and dry forest.

As he ran, Neal kept reliving last night over and over in his mind, trying to think of something he may have missed. Everyone was saying that the lights were probably an enemy tactic, but they had come from south of the camp—the direction opposite the battlefront. How could they have been caused by the enemy?

He envisioned Becca getting struck by the lightning again. Remembered the terror he had felt as he watched her fly through the air and collapse in a limp huddle on the ground. Her pale face as he realized she wasn't breathing. The feeling like he himself couldn't breathe. But the lights… they had disappeared. When? He couldn't remember exactly. Sometime after a bright flash. He'd been so fixed on Becca.

Neal panted as the path before him got steeper. He would talk to Becca later. For now, he needed to focus.

Chapter Six

Finally, the day came to an end and Neal found himself at their dining table once again. Matt and Nick sat down next to him, Lizzy and Ruth opposite. The five of them tucked in, hoping that Officer Mains hadn't been put on dinner duty today. He always undercooked the meat.

"So, are you going to visit her tonight?" Matt asked Neal as he gave his meat a curious sniff.

"Probably," Neal said.

"Good," Lizzy said. "I want to come too." She reached over and quickly scooped a chunk of potatoes from Nick's tray. Nick tried to stop her, but she was too fast. She wiggled her eyebrows at him as she licked her spoon clean. Nick glared back.

Neal nodded at Lizzy. "Yeah, she'd probably like that."

"Thank God we get the rest of the night off," Nick said, now throwing a green bean at Lizzy. "If we had to do more drills tonight, I think I'd collapse."

The others agreed.

"The funny thing is," Ruth said quietly, "Becca's going to be so mad that she missed today."

"She's insane," Nick said with a shake of his head.

The others grinned and said little else as they scarfed down their food to quell their aching stomachs. Fifteen minutes later Sergeant Nelson stood up. As always, everyone stopped eating and stood at attention. Once he left, they disposed of their trays and filed out of the room. The loud rumble of tired voices drifted up to the second floor, where almost everyone either went back to their bunks to lie down or to the rec room or play some cards. Neal and Lizzy, however, peeled off from the group and pointed their feet in the direction of the hospital.

They were silent as they walked through the large double doors to the hospital wing, weaving their way through the office-filled hallways. Neal's mind was still reeling, searching for some sort of answer. He felt a gentle punch on his arm and looked down at Lizzy.

"She's going to be okay, you know. The doctor's not worried, and we've seen her make it through worse pain," she said.

"I know," he sighed. "It's just, I can't stop picturing her getting struck and..." He trailed off, not knowing how to describe the horror he had felt as she lay there motionless.

Lizzy nodded and said nothing else. They walked through two security doors and down a clean hallway. When they passed through the doors of the hospital, Neal noted that more of the soldiers were up and about now; the nurses seemed to be working wonders. It wasn't hard for him to find Becca. She was still in the bed where he had laid her that morning, and, as predicted, she didn't look very happy. Neal and Lizzy glanced at each other, then went over to her bed.

"Hey, Becca," Lizzy chirped. "How are you feeling?"

"Fine, I guess. I can't believe they've had me stuck here all day. They won't let me get up! Well, unless I have to go to the bathroom, so I've said I've had to go about twenty times today. I think that nurse is about ready to wring my neck," she said, nodding at a nurse helping to rewrap a soldier's wounds five beds down.

Lizzy laughed.

"Sounds like you're doing alright, then?" Neal asked, smiling.

Becca looked up at him and gave a small smile in return. "Yeah, worrywart, I'm fine."

"Does your head still hurt?" Lizzy asked.

"Not so much," she replied, now avoiding eye contact.

Neal's eyebrows creased. He wasn't sure he believed her, but Lizzy smiled and started telling her about how hard they had been drilled that day.

70

Becca listened eagerly and continuously interrupted with shouts of exasperation at having missed out. Neal didn't listen; his eye had been caught by the movement down the opposite wall of beds. A nurse was pulling open some curtains, which only a moment before had blocked Dr. Rosner and an injured soldier from view.

When Dr. Rosner had patted the man on the shoulder and turned away, Neal's stomach flipped over. It was Ed Adams. Worry about Becca was wiped from his mind as he stared.

He's right there, and he knows about Finn...

Neal looked back at Becca and Lizzy, who were still chatting happily. But suddenly it seemed like they were at the end of a long tunnel, unfocused, their voices echoing from a distance. He looked at Adams again. His mind was reeling, but he clenched his jaw and gathered his resolve.

I'm doing this.

He gave the girls a nod to signal that he would be right back, then quickly moved across the ward. With every step, he felt a knot grow in his stomach. He had no idea what he was going to say to Adams, but he knew that if he didn't do this now, he would chicken out and never talk to him.

Adams looked up as Neal approached his bed. Surprise spread over his face and he got a little paler, but at least he was definitely all here this time. Stopping at the side of the bed, Neal nodded awkwardly.

"Hi," he said. "I'm—"

"Neal Donahue." Ed Adams nodded. "Yeah, you look a lot like your brother."

Neal swallowed dryly. He wasn't sure what to say to that. "How... how are you?" he asked, glancing at the bandage wrap around Adams' middle.

"I'll heal. Then I'll probably be right back out there."

"My friend Matt said that might happen for a lot of you."

"Smart kid," Adams replied. He gave Neal an appraising look. "I know you're not just here to check up on me, though. You want to ask about Finn."

The knot in Neal's stomach tightened and he nodded silently. The reality that he was about to find out what happened to Finn was hitting him, and he felt like he was back in that moment two years ago when Sergeant Nelson informed him of his brother's death.

"Sit down, kid," Adams said, gesturing to an empty chair nearby. "You look like you're about to give out."

Neal brought the chair over to Adams' bed, sat down nervously, and tried to stop his hands from shaking.

"How well did you know Finn?" Neal asked.

"Well enough," Adams said. "We trained here for three years, then were sent out in the same regiment to fight at the front. Your brother was a good soldier."

Neal nodded. "How long were you at the front?"

Adams scanned Neal's face. "Five months, you didn't know that?"

"We never even heard that Finn had been sent to the front," Neal said with a small shake of his head.

Adams rubbed his chin. "I'm sorry, it must have come as a real shock. He was a good fighter, though. Your family has a lot to be proud of. Still, it didn't prepare me for what he did when he... you know."

Neal leaned forward in his seat. "What did he do?" he asked nervously. "What happened that day?"

Adams regarded Neal carefully, a sadness in his eyes. "You sure you want to hear this, kid?"

Neal hesitated a second, then pushed away any lingering doubts and nodded. He had to know what happened to Finn.

"Okay then," Adams sighed. "Well, your brother and I were both part of the 402nd regiment. We were sent forward with three other regiments to make a big push into the Lossian Nation. It was a long five months, but eventually we were able to push Sarlic's troops out of the Edscaftian Nation and deeper into the Lossian Nation than our military had pushed them in years...

73

Which is saying something. Sarlic Lossi and his army are no joke. Well, you know for yourself how they tear apart the lands they cross and what they do to the people who don't escape in time..."

Adams shuddered. "It's not something you can forget in a hurry — Anyway, we pushed the Lossians back into their lands, all the way to Maytown. We were told that we once we took Maytown, we would be able to establish a base. You see, the city has connections to some of the most important rivers and roads in the Lossian Nation. Taking this city would be a huge blow to Sarlic. And our strategy was working... until it wasn't.

"We managed to push them deep into the city. Half of it was ours, and it looked like we were actually going to be able to take it."

Adams stopped; his face twisted with the pain of the memory. Whatever he had seen that day must have been horrible, and Neal didn't want to push him... but he had to know what happened to Finn. He waited awkwardly for Adams to continue, gripping the edges of the chair so hard his knuckles turned white.

"It was a trap," Adams sighed as he passed his hands over his eyes. "They had lured us into one of their toughest strongholds, and before we knew what was happening, we were completely surrounded. The Lossians had set up blockades and tanks at all the important intersections of the city. Their soldiers were everywhere. Stationed at every street, on every building... they cornered us in the town square. They started picking us off faster than we could run. There was no way out. Three hundred of us, trapped…"

Adams looked up at Neal, who saw the pain swimming in his eyes. "I thought we were all going to die that day, but your brother—"

Neal caught his breath.

"He did something so *stupid*… none of us would be here without him."

Adams sighed and adjusted his position with a small grunt of pain. Then he continued.

"Sarlic's men were closing in. Everywhere I looked there were bullets, falling soldiers, explosions. The screams—" Adams voice shook as he continued. "We lost a lot of good soldiers that day. And I could hear the Lossians…laughing."

Neal waited for Adams to continue.

"It didn't look good, but Finn saw something. I'm not sure what. He muttered something to me and pointed over at the Lossians. To this day I'm not sure what he said or what was pointing at, but before I could ask him, he took off.

"Your brother sprinted right into the thick of the fight. I shouted after him, but he didn't listen, he just kept running. I lost him in the smog. I don't know where he went Neal, I thought he was gone. The battle got worse, a lot worse," Adams whispered. "I was convinced it was over, there was no way out kid — they had us lock and barrel. Then the next thing I knew one of their tanks turned on them and fired a blast. Its missile went flying straight to the heart of the Lossians' thickest blockade, behind which must have been rows and rows of ammunition. The blast was deafening, and it felt as though the world was being torn apart.

"Then, Kober was shouting through the mess and ordering us through the destroyed blockade, out into safety. Your brother had taken over that tank. He saved hundreds of soldiers' lives, but the tank was situated too close to the explosion... He didn't make it."

Neal stared at Adams' pale countenance. The wounded soldier was looking determinedly at his trembling hands, but Neal knew he could see every inch of that bloody scene just as clearly in his mind's eye. Neal slowly unstuck his own hands from the side of his chair and let out an unsteady breath. Part of him couldn't believe Adams' tale, the other part didn't doubt it for a moment. His insides felt like they were writhing, and his head was buzzing numbly.

Neal couldn't think of anything to say. What could he say to someone who watched his brother die? Someone who had lived through something like that? Should he thank Adams for reliving such a horrible moment just so he could learn what happened to his brother? Slowly, he stood up and placed his hand on Ed Adams' shoulder.

Adams looked up at him. The two nodded at each other, and Neal knew Adams understood.

"If you're anything like Finn," Adams said, "you'll make a good soldier."

Neal tried to say something, but no noise would come out. Adams held out his hand. Neal shook it, and Adams gave him a small smile.

"I'll see you around, kid."

Again, Neal nodded. Then he let go and turned away.

Walking very slowly, Neal made his way back over to Becca's bed. Lizzy was still updating Becca on everything that had happened today. Neal joined them silently, but didn't hear a thing they were saying.

His gaze lingered on Becca, but only saw images of the battle Adams had described. Becca had said that knowing might not make things better. He had refused to believe her at the time... but now he realized she had a point.

Lizzy laughed loudly at something Becca said, pulling Neal back to the present. He shook his head to clear it and looked shrewdly at Becca. She was laughing too, but he could tell she was faking. She looked more like she was trying not to be sick than anything else. Concerned, Neal raised himself on his toes just enough to see the other side of her bed. There was a bucket nearby, its handle pointed up so that she could easily grab it. Looking back at Becca, he studied her face. She was still really pale and she was sweating; she almost looked feverish.

She's been sick all day! Neal mentally kicked himself for not noticing sooner. He had let himself get distracted, when it was Becca he had come to see in the first place.

He glanced over at the nurse Becca had mentioned earlier and noticed that she did keep eyeing Becca, but not with exasperation.

"This is ridiculous!" Becca shouted, calling Neal's attention back to her. She threw her arms up in frustration as she said, "I should be out there with you guys. I'm fine. I need to be ready to face the enemy too!"

Neal said nothing, but watched as she placed her hands back down on the bed. They were shaking slightly. Lizzy laughed again, and glanced over her shoulder as a soldier limped by.

"I think I helped to bring him in yesterday," she said absently.

While she was looking away Becca closed her eyes tightly and took a deep breath. Neal reached down and gently placed his hand on her arm. She looked up at him, no longer trying to hide the pain. He gave her a reassuring nod.

"Hey, Lizzy," he said.

"Yeah?" Lizzy said, turning back around.

"I think we should get going, Becca probably wants to annoy the nurse one last time tonight."

Lizzy turned back to Becca. "Well, alright, if you must," she said. She reached down and gave Becca a quick hug. "You'll be out there with us soon. Until then, I'll make sure Nick gets pushed hard enough to cover your work too," Lizzy said with a wink.

Becca laughed and gave them a little wave as Neal and Lizzy turned away. When they got to the door, Neal held it open for Lizzy and glanced back at Becca. She had her head in her hands, and the nurse was running over to her side.

Neal followed Lizzy into the hall.

"See, nothing to worry about," Lizzy said, giving him a gentle shove.

Neal forced a smile. "I guess you were right."

Lizzy led the way cheerfully upstairs and to the other end of the building. Neal trudged behind, his mind swimming with the story Adams had told him and no less relieved of his worries for Becca. It didn't seem like they had made any progress with her headache. Really, it seemed like things were worse. It was just a headache, shouldn't that be something easy to solve? Neal sighed, and looked up as they entered the rec room.

The rec room was a sprawling space with red carpet and a few windows that were closer to the ceiling than they were to the floor. Nearest the door where Neal and Lizzy had walked in was an assortment of large stuffed chairs. At some point they had probably been arranged nicely, but they had been moved around so many times that no one could remember where they originally belonged. There were many wooden tables scattered about the room too. These were used for card games, letter writing, arm wrestling, and even studying. Although, just about everyone refrained from studying in here. At the far end of the room were a few bookshelves and cabinets full of cards, balls, darts, and whatever else anyone might want to use. A single radio was set up next to the last cabinet, and it was often spouting off updates about the war. Only when someone declared that they couldn't listen to the updates any longer was the station changed to play music. Every song they heard was decades old, as no one had recorded any new music in years.

Almost everyone stationed at Dune Hills seemed to be crammed into the room tonight. Neal and Lizzy sifted through the crowd as they made their way over to Matt, Ruth, and Nick, who were talking quietly in a few of the chairs. The three of them looked up at Neal and Lizzy as they sat down. Their expressions made it clear that they all wanted to know how Becca was doing.

"She's pretty good," Lizzy announced. "You were right about her being upset about being stuck there, but she seems to be making the most of it. Honestly, I don't think they'll keep her in there very long."

Nick let out a deep breath. "Great," he said. "Want to arm wrestle?"

"Nick!" Ruth chided.

"You're on!" Lizzy answered, jumping back out of her chair.

With that Nick and Lizzy set off for one of the tables, each claiming that the other was about face the shame of losing. Matt shook his head and turned back to Neal.

"So that's it? She's alright, just like that?" he said.

Neal shrugged. "She says she's alright, but she didn't look too good. The nurse that was watching her seemed on edge too. I'm not sure they know what's wrong with her."

Matt and Ruth looked at each other, worry passing over their faces.

"I'm sure Dr. Rosner will figure out what's going on," Ruth said uncertainly.

Neal ran his fingers through his hair. "Yeah well, let's hope so."

"I'll look up what I can in the medical books here," Matt offered. "Maybe an extra set of eyes will help Dr. Rosner find an answer sooner."

"Right," Ruth said, giving Neal's hand a gentle squeeze. "I'm sure we'll figure out what's going on in no time."

Neal smiled and nodded halfheartedly, then slouched back in his chair, letting his head slide down to rest on the top of it. Gazing up at the plain ceiling, he tried not to let himself worry about Becca. He could feel Matt and Ruth watching him for a moment, but then they went back to their conversation. Matt was telling Ruth more about his time at the front. Any other time, Neal would have been interested to know too, but right now he didn't think he could stomach it. A loud cheer came from the other side of the room. It sounded like Nick and Lizzy had attracted an audience.

Neal closed his eyes and let the rush of sounds wash over him. He was exhausted, emotionally and physically, and he surprised himself by realizing he wished Becca was here to talk about it. The way Matt and Ruth were talking. He opened his eyes and looked at the two of them. They seemed happy. He knew Matt and Ruth had a thing for each other; it had been that way for a long time. Maybe now that Matt was back, something would happen. But he and Becca? Neal pushed the thought away. Another loud cheer interrupted his thoughts, and then Lizzy crowed loudly at Nick. Neal closed his eyes again, trying to clear his mind. But just as he managed to relax, radio commentary came pouring into the room.

"We have received confirmation that the Edscaftian Council has approved the relocation of three more villages," said the reporter. "Councilman Valdez released this statement earlier today: 'The safety of the people of the Edscaftian Nation is still the Council's number-one concern. We will do whatever it takes to ensure our civilians remain safe against the continued attacks of Sarlic Lossi. He started this war by sowing hate and disunity within the Edscaftian Nation. He tore the North away to create the Lossian Nation, and attacked us because we would not condone his treasonous acts or meet his villainous demands. We will not let further acts of disunity break us. The Edscaftian Council is working hard to keep you and every other member of this Nation safe as we continue to search for a way to end this war. The Council is sending more of our soldiers to the villages nearest the front to help with the evacuation. We are asking citizens of the nearest cities to show your generosity once more by helping these families find somewhere safe to stay during the relocation.'

"While some may find the Council's continued focus on the safety of our villages comforting, new concerns are rattling the rest of us. The Council has yet to answer our most pressing questions. Many individuals throughout the Nation have come forward saying that they spotted strange and unusual lights lighting up the sky only last night."

Neal bolted up, listening more closely.

"While many theories are already being tossed around regarding the origin of these lights, the Council has yet to even acknowledge the lights' existence. When approached for questioning earlier today, Councilwoman Sparks said, 'The Council doubts that any such lights truly exist. Rumors of similar sightings fill the history books, but have never been proven. Those who claim to have seen any bright lights filling the sky likely mistook the moonlight hitting the clouds on a clear night. It is useless for the Council to waste time on matters such as these. We have a war to worry about and a Nation to protect.'"

Neal looked over at Matt and Ruth, who had stopped their conversation to listen as well. They shared a skeptical look but kept their ears perked as the reporter continued.

"While the Council may be taking an offhand approach to the mysterious lights of last night, many have expressed worries that these lights may indeed have a connection to the war, even to Sarlic Lossi himself. Rumors of a new weapon invented by none other than Lossi have been circulating for some time. Many worry that these lights may be from said weapon..."

"Is that why we're not allowed to talk about the lights here?" Neal asked Ruth and Matt. "The Council is trying to hush it up?"

"I don't see why, though," Ruth said. "Won't refusing to acknowledge it just cause more panic?"

"Maybe they're hoping that if they sound unconcerned about it, the people won't worry about it," Matt said.

"But why say that the lights don't exist?" Neal persisted. "They clearly do. *I* saw them, and there is no way they were some reflection of the moon. I've never seen colors light up the sky the way these lights did."

"Well, maybe they—"

"What are you three up to?" interrupted a voice above them.

Neal, Matt, and Ruth looked up to see one of the drill sergeants standing over them. His face was stern, and his eyes flickered over the three of them, then to the radio, which was still spouting the evening report.

"Many are worried that these lights may affect..."

The drill sergeant marched over and turned the radio off with a sharp click.

"You three should get to bed," he said. "You look exhausted."

Neal, Matt, and Ruth shared another look.

"We've got a long day ahead of us tomorrow, you'll want to be well rested," he insisted.

"Yes, sir," the three of them replied.

He nodded at them as they slowly stood up. They moved quietly away from their corner of the rec room and hurried toward the door, feeling his stare on their backs. As they wove through a group of older soldiers who were arguing about best firearm ready positions, Neal glanced back. The drill sergeant was still watching them. Neal quickly turned around and hurried after the others.

"How long do you think he was listening?" Ruth whispered as they slowly walked down the hall.

"Clearly long enough to hear us talking about" —Matt glanced over his shoulder and lowered his voice—"the lights."

"All this secrecy around the lights is making me wonder…" Ruth trailed off and glanced at Neal nervously.

"Wonder if Becca is worse off than we thought?" he asked, avoiding her gaze.

"Yeah," Ruth whispered.

They stopped walking and looked down the stairs which would take them down to the hospital wing.

"If it was bad, we would know, right?" she asked.

Matt put his arm around Ruth's shoulder. "Right," he said. "If they were worried about something serious. I mean, you were there too, Neal. They'd probably be worried whatever affected her had some sort of residual effect on you too."

Neal nodded absently. "Yeah, they'd be pulling both of us out of here if they were really worried." He turned and led the way to the dormitories. "Come on, we should get to bed before the drill sergeant comes to check on us."

Chapter Seven

After a night full of nightmares about Becca turning into a poisonous gas and killing everyone in their camp, Neal woke with the ominous feeling that day was going to be just as awful as the last. Unfortunately, he soon found he was right. At breakfast it was announced over the sound of the pouring rain that three of the wounded soldiers had passed away overnight. A dull gloom hung over the camp as the drill sergeants pushed them hard from dawn until dusk, and once again no one was good enough.

As the long day drew to a close, there was a procession held for the fallen soldiers. Their bodies were respectfully placed onto trucks to be transferred to their families. Neal watched the caskets as they were carried past, and visions of what Finn's last moments must have been like flashed in his mind, followed closely by his own memories of the day he had been told of Finn's death, and the family visit he had been allowed to take.

He saw himself arriving at the train station where his distraught older sister Caitlin picked him up. Saw his mother's red and puffy eyes when he arrived back home at their farm, and his dad sitting deathly quiet out in their field, looking lost. He remembered his younger siblings not fully understanding what had happened, his other sisters bursting into tears during dinner, and the floor-dropping emptiness that he had felt... that he still felt whenever he thought of his brother. And then he remembered another feeling. That fierce determination to go back and train harder so that no member of his family would ever have to feel pain like that again.

Neal suddenly found that he wanted nothing else but to hug his mother and see his siblings again. Blinking fiercely, he followed his regiment back inside the camp.

This war has to end, he thought. *No one else should feel that. No one else should be separated from their families.*

As he made his way through the front doors, Neal intended to go visit Becca again, but Sergeant Nelson announced that lights out was in twenty minutes. So, he followed the others back to the dormitories and fell asleep more homesick than he had felt in a long time.

The next day was tough as well, but when it finally ended Neal decided to skip dinner and go visit Becca. Exhausted as he was, he was dying to talk to her and didn't want to miss this chance. When he was standing next to her again, he was saddened to see that she didn't look any better, and hesitated. He wasn't sure if it was a good idea to trouble her.

"What?" Becca said, cocking her head at him. "You can tell me. What is it?"

Neal still hesitated.

"It'll take my mind off the pain," she coaxed.

Neal sighed and sat down on the edge of her bed. "Okay. Well, the thing is, I talked to Adams…"

He told her everything. First the story of Finn's death, and then what he and the others had heard on the radio about the lights, as well as the mystifying behavior of all the commanding officers at the camp.

"They pop up anytime one of us even tries to talk about the lights and tell us to stop, and I'm not sure why," Neal whispered. "They must know more than they're letting on, which makes me nervous. What if—"

"Neal," Becca interrupted. "Stop."

Neal looked up at her as she placed her shaking hand on top of his. She was giving him the same concerned look he often directed at her.

"Why did you ask Adams about your brother?" she asked.

"I had to," he shrugged. "I had to know what happened. I had to know why he was taken away from us."

She raised her eyebrows. "Us?"

"My family," he mumbled while shifting his gaze out the window. "Why we were, well... broken."

She made a small noise and he looked at her again, but her face was blank.

"And so, what? You're better now?" she asked.

Neal didn't say anything. He knew what she was getting at. She had said before that knowing wouldn't help, but she didn't understand. She didn't know what it felt like to lose an older brother and not know why. Not know why he had been taken away without even getting to say goodbye. She didn't know what it felt like to imagine going home again and realize that it would never be as perfect as it was before. That Finn was never going to be there again.

Before Neal knew what was happening, Becca was putting her arms around him. She didn't say anything, and she didn't ask him to say anymore. She just hugged him, burying her face in his shoulder. Neal hugged her back and the two held onto each other tightly. All the worries of the past few days seemed to fade, and he hugged her tighter. For a moment they stayed like that, and Neal let the rest of the world slip away.

Then Becca have a sharp lurch and pulled herself away. She yanked the bucket off the ground and with a crashing blow of reality heaved up what little was in her stomach. The nurse came rushing over and pushed Neal out of the ward, telling him that Becca needed to rest. Neal left, and all of the worries of the past few days came flooding back.

***

The next few weeks passed much the same. The regiments at Dune Hills were pushed to practice their shooting, dodging, and battle tactics day after day. When they weren't doing that, they were ordered to study maps and accounts of past battles. If they studied the mistakes made in past battles, they were told, they would be less likely to make the same ones when sent out. A few nights a week there was night training. They ran through the forest in teams, learning how to move as quietly as possible in the dark and implementing some of their battle tactics, although most of the time they failed miserably at their objectives. When they weren't doing that, they were set on night watch.

There were no more signs of the lights since the night Becca had been struck, and they still weren't permitted to talk about them. Neal kept an eye out for them when on night watch, but he didn't see so much as a shooting star, let alone a bright stream of colorful lights.

Becca still hadn't gotten any better. Neal went to visit her as often as he could, sometimes bringing Lizzy, Matt, Ruth, or Nick with him, but sitting at her bedside wasn't doing any good. Ruth kept saying Dr. Rosner would figure out what was going on with Becca any day now, but as the weeks dragged by Neal became more certain that the doctor had no idea what was wrong with her. As promised, Matt was digging through one medical volume after another, hoping to find something that might connect to her symptoms, but nothing he found seemed to make any sense.

Neal often went to the library himself, seeking information on the lights. Despite his efforts, he couldn't find even a mention of them. He tore through both history and science books for any clue as to what the lights were, what might have caused them, or where they had come from. But he wasn't having any luck. Until something caught his eye one day after a particularly discouraging visit to the hospital.

Neal was scanning a book that dictated the early history of the Edscaftian Nation and was halfway through a chapter discussing the legends of the great warriors who had helped to found their Nation when he saw it. Down near the bottom of the page, the author was reviewing a legend Neal had heard hundreds of times before.

Many speak of the great strength of the warriors who founded our Nation, and rely on their stories to encourage the same virtue in their own children. It is a testament to this strength that these warriors united many peoples of neighboring lands under the Edscaftian Council. Tales have been passed down from generation to generation regarding not only the forming of our Nation but even our Founding Day itself. A rare few of these tales mention a strange and most likely fictitious sight marking that night: They claim that the sky glowed brightly with a river of light which—

Neal turned the page so quickly that he almost ripped it, then stared in disbelief. The other side of the page had been completely blacked out and the rest of the chapter was gone, ripped out from the binding. Neal picked the book up and looked at the page more closely, holding it up to the light, straining to read through the black ink. However, the words behind the ink had been lost to time, along with any answers he might have found about the lights. Neal gave a grunt of frustration and threw the book across the table. Why were they being so secretive about these lights? What was the Council trying to hide from them?

The lack of answers regarding all of these questions did anything but soothe Neal's nerves as his worries about Becca steadily increased. She had gotten thin and pale, and she was always shivering. From what he could find out from the nurse, she was throwing up multiple times a day and the pounding in her head wasn't getting any better. A few of the times he had visited her, Neal had noticed a tissue or a scrap of her leftover food float weirdly in the air after she touched it. He still wasn't sure of what he was seeing, however, so he kept it to himself, wondering if that too had anything to do with the lights. Neal decided to expand his search for anything that might cause this reaction, but still he had no luck.

To top all of this off, new reports were coming in that things were getting uglier at the front. Hospitals were being overrun with wounded soldiers, and calls were going out for more volunteers to help treat them. Rumors floated throughout the camp about the injuries these soldiers had been inflicted with, all of which pointed at the fact that Sarlic Lossi had become more brutal in his war tactics. His escalating anger was flooding into his troops, and the Edscaftian military was feeling the effects. Over the weeks Neal counted seven soldiers in Dune Hills who were pulled aside and informed of a relative who had died in battle.

As the battle pushed farther into their lands, more Edscaftian villages had been abandoned, forcing families out of their homes and deeper into the safety of their Nation. Ruth in particular took this news badly as they sat listening to the radio in the rec room.

"I can't believe it," she said from the table she was sitting at. "Those poor families. I hope they all make it to safety."

"Of course they will," said Nick. "All they have to do is get out in time. There can't be any real danger in that, right?"

Ruth glared at Nick while Matt, Neal, and Lizzy erupted in indignation.

"No real danger?" Matt shouted down at him from his perch on top of a pile of chairs. "Are you kidding me, Nick? Take that back right now!"

"What?"

"You know that Ruth and her brothers lost their parents when they had to flee their village," Lizzy snapped at him.

Nick looked over at Ruth, who was still glaring at him, a bit paler than before. He blushed furiously. "Sorry, Ruth," he mumbled. "I didn't think... I'm sorry."

"It's fine," Ruth said in a quiet voice. "It was a long time ago." She then turned back to the letter she was writing to her older brothers while Nick watched her uncomfortably.

The group sat quietly for a while, still listening to the radio as the noise in the room grew steadily louder. Some of the guys had decided to have a wrestling match, so the chairs and tables had been pushed to the farthest walls, and now two large guys were tumbling on the red carpet beneath them, taunting each other while everyone else cheered them on. Finally, Nick and Lizzy had heard enough from the radio, so they got up for a better view of the wrestling match.

Neal sat quietly in his chair hardly paying attention to the noise around him. With everything that had been going on lately, he was in a pretty suppressed mood. He just wanted one piece of good news—preferably that Becca was getting better.

"Hey, Neal!" Matt called, over the din of the wrestling match.

Neal looked up. Matt had laid his medical book open in his lap and was looking down at him with a grin on his still scruffy face.

"What's up?"

"I think your sister's here!"

Neal started up. Making his way along the edge of the wall, he climbed on top of Ruth's table next to Matt's perch and looked out of the window. It had a clear view of the courtyard, which was well lit by the lamps on the surrounding walls. Two soldiers were jogging down the steps, heading straight for a military car that had just pulled in. Other officers were already at the back of a truck parked close to the building, pulling out supplies. Next to the car stood its driver and a woman whose auburn hair was pulled back in a tight bun, a large mail sack hanging at her side.

Neal recognized her immediately. Reaching up, he gave Matt a grateful pat on the leg and jumped down from the table. Pushing past the others and stepping over a few legs in the process, Neal made it to the door of the rec room and turned right down the hall. He leapt down the stairs and trotted the rest of the way to the mail room. He passed several soldiers walking by with the boxes of supplies, then moved through a door on his left. He scanned the room for his sister, but she wasn't there. More soldiers came in, and Neal moved out of the way. He waited patiently, knowing she would be back soon. He was right—hardly a moment later the tall, sturdy form of his sister came through the door.

"Caitlin!" Neal greeted.

Caitlin's head snapped up, then her face broke into a wide, warm smile. Neal made his way over to her and the two embraced in a warm hug. Stepping back, they looked at each other, Caitlin looking up slightly.

"Well, I guess I'm not taller than you anymore," Caitlin said.

Neal smiled. "I guess not. How have you been? How is everyone? How are things out there? Have you heard any updates about the front? Where are all the families being located to?"

"Whoa, whoa, slow down, little brother, one question at a time."

"Sorry, it's just—"

"I know, it's been a while." Caitlin nodded. "Just give me a sec, I need to finish distributing all the mail, then we can talk. We won't have too long, though. The truck will be leaving again in about forty-five minutes."

Neal nodded and, looking around, found a seat nearby. He waited for Caitlin to finish her job, watching as more boxes were taken in and out. Finally, she came hurrying back into the room.

"Done," came her greeting as she threw herself into a chair next to Neal. "So, how's my little brother doing? I'm not going to lie, you're looking pretty big. They must be working you hard."

Neal laughed. "You don't know the half of it. I'm alright I suppose. Really there's not much to tell here."

Caitlin raised her eyebrow. "Not much to tell? Okay then, how's Becca?"

Neal felt himself turn red. "She's fine."

"Oh, I'm sure. Only fine. And spending every day with her is also just fine?"

His neck got even hotter. "Yeah well, actually she's pretty sick. She hasn't been out of the hospital in about a month."

"What? Are you serious? What happened? What's wrong with her?"

"We're not allowed to talk about it," Neal mumbled.

Caitlin stared at him for a moment, studying his worried face. "I'm sure she'll be alright," she said bracingly. "I mean, she's Becca after all, isn't she? I thought she was the toughest, most amazing girl around?" she added with a sly smirk.

"I... I've never said that. Why would you— Well, how's Tod then?" he asked in an effort to change the subject with a pointed glance at Caitlin's ring-less left hand.

This time it was Caitlin's turn to blush. "Tod is fine," she said with a small smile, sliding her hand out of Neal's sight. "He's the lead assistant at the weapons engineering camp, so I haven't seen him in a while."

He nodded, grinning. "How's the outside?" he asked again. "We've heard some reports about hospitals filling up and more families being forced out of their homes."

Her smile faded. "Yeah, it's as ugly as they say. I stopped by a hospital the other day... Those poor soldiers. The rumors about Sarlic's new weapon and new tactics must be true, I haven't ever seen wounds like these before. And people are positively pouring in from the front. Even the

98

villages who haven't been affected yet are evacuating, no one is sure how long they'll be safe. Not to mention we've recently heard some strange reports about accidents and missing persons lately."

"What?" Neal leaned forward in his seat.

"A few soldiers have gone missing that were reportedly safe in their camp one day and the next... gone. And there have been some strange reports coming in about things no one has been able to explain. Some of the accidents were too deep into our Nation for the Council's comfort. They're investigating, but everyone is worried the Lossians have infiltrated some of our bases."

He let out a low whistle. "Any back this far?" he asked quietly.

She shook her head. "They're all rumors, Neal," she said. "And no, there have been no rumors about Dune Hills."

"How come things have turned bad so quickly? Do you know what's changing?" he asked.

"No idea," she said. "But that's not all. Since the fighting has gotten so nasty lately, Sarlic Lossi and his military have been pushing our soldiers back and we can't seem to regain the ground. They've started pushing us back towards the High Rise River, and if they get much farther—"

"Are you serious?" Neal blurted. "The war hasn't been pushed that far back in *twelve years*!"

"I know. It's bad." Caitlin looked at him very seriously. "Just be careful, okay? If things keep going like this, you guys might be called forward sooner than you think, and if you're called up..."

Neal took in the anxiety on her face. "I know, I'll be careful."

"Good. You better."

"How are Mom and Dad and everyone?" Neal asked, ignoring her half-stern, half-amused look.

Caitlin smiled. "Good. Mom and Dad are holding out the best they can, you know them. They never really stop moving. And everyone is helping out in any way *they* can." She started counting off their siblings on her fingers. "Nora is now a secretary for the Edscaftian Council. That's why I know as much as I do." She winked.

Neal smiled and shook his head.

"Kelly is helping Dad out with the farm, and they're sending a lot of the crops over to the nearest food collection bank. The bank is sending it over to the soldiers at the front. Brigid started helping Mom out at the hospital about a month ago, now she's finally old enough. I guess she's been driving Mom up the wall asking when she could go help. And Freya and Owen are holding down the fort at home. Oh! You'll love this! The other day when Kelly and Dad came back from the field they found Freya and Owen chasing the chickens through an obstacle course they had set up with the hay bales."

He chuckled, then sighed. "Ah, I miss those two. I miss all you guys."

"Well, make sure you send a letter home then," Caitlin said. "Everyone misses you too, and they'd be thrilled if you sent them something. I could even deliver it."

Neal leaned in. "Actually, there was something I wanted to tell you."

"What is it?"

"I talked to Ed Adams," he said in a rush.

Caitlin's face went pale. "You... you what?"

"He's here," he hurried on. "We brought him back from the front a while back and I had a chance to talk to him and ask about what happened the day that... that Finn..."

Caitlin opened her mouth to say something, but nothing came out.

"Do you want to hear what he said?" Neal asked.

Caitlin hesitated for a moment, then nodded.

"Okay," Neal said, and took a deep breath.

He repeated Adams' story, trying his best to remember every detail. He also described how Adams had acted while telling it, to give Caitlin the full picture.

"It must have been really bad," he finished quietly. "From the way Adams looked, I'm sure it was a day he'd rather never have to remember again. But Finn saved them. He helped them all escape."

Tears were streaming down Caitlin's face. "I'm glad you talked to him," she choked out. "It'll mean a lot to Mom and Dad to hear that he died a hero."

Neal nodded, and wiped away a few tears of his own.

She gave him a small, watery smile. "We're all really proud of you, you know. That you stayed in the military even after Finn died."

He nodded and looked down at his hands. "Yeah well, look what this war has done to our family... to everyone's families..."

Caitlin put her hand over his. "We'll all be together again soon, I'm sure we will."

Neal looked up at his sister. She was trying to comfort him, the way she would have when they were little and he was hurt. But he could tell that she wasn't as certain as her words. How could she be? It was more likely that they were all going to die than be reunited.

"Yeah," he said. "I'm sure we'll find a way to push Sarlic back soon."

Caitlin gave his hand a small squeeze, then checked her watch. "Oh no, is that the time? I should really get going. They'll want to be heading off soon."

"Yeah, okay."

Getting up, the two of them hugged each other tightly. "Are you sure you're doing alright?" she asked, taking in his face again.

"Yeah," he said. "I'm fine, they just keep us busy is all."

Caitlin looked doubtful, but nodded. "Okay then. Well, say hi to Becca for me. I'll be sure to pass on what you told me to Mom and Dad, and I'll tell them you send your love and all that, and keep me posted on any transfers that you get, alright?"

Neal grinned. "You got it."

Turning, the two of them headed out of the room, down the hallway to the main entrance, and out into the courtyard. Already, the truck that Caitlin had arrived in was holding another load of boxes and barrels. They stepped to the side to get out of the way of the few last boxes, then looked toward the door as Sergeant Nelson came walking down with the head officers who had arrived with Caitlin. He was looking serious as the officers whispered hurriedly in his ear; whatever they were saying didn't appear to be good news.

Neal saluted and stood at attention as Sergeant Nelson walked by. The sergeant returned with a distracted salute and continued on. Watching them go, Neal caught Caitlin's eye.

"What?"

She smiled. "Nothing."

Shaking his head, Neal looked away and watched as the last of the soldiers loaded their crates onto the truck. "You should probably get over there," he said.

"Yeah," Caitlin replied, turning to him one last time. "You'll keep in touch?"

"Of course."

The two quickly hugged, then Caitlin ran off to the truck and slid into the front bench. Shortly after, the other officers filed into the military car and circled out the gate. The truck followed suit, slowly backing up, swinging around, and taking off down the road, where it was quickly swallowed up by the mouth of the night. Neal watched until the gates slammed shut behind them. Then he turned and made to walk back up the stairs—when he saw Sergeant Nelson staring at him. Neal nodded awkwardly. Sergeant Nelson did the same, then went inside. Neal waited for him to disappear before he followed, hoping that the Edscaftian Nation really could find a way to keep fighting off Lossi and stop him from taking any more of their land.

Chapter Eight

The hospital ward was quiet, as most of the soldiers were asleep. A few of them were muttering or groaning, haunted by memories of the battlefield. One sounded like he was crying. Pulling her pillow up, Becca slid her head underneath it. She knew she should sleep, but the sounds of these soldiers' nightmares weren't helping. Night after night, they had whimpered, or yelled, or screamed while thrashing on their beds. At first, it had put Becca on edge, wondering what they were seeing or reliving that was making them act that way. She was no longer surprised by their outbursts, but that didn't make them any easier to ignore.

The pillow wasn't working, so Becca sighed, rolled onto her back, and placed her head back on top of the pillow. She stared at the ceiling and wondered how much longer they were going to make her stay here. It had been a month, and they still weren't any closer to figuring out what was wrong with her.

She glanced down at the bucket next to her bed and shuddered as a sickening feeling rose up the back of her throat. She quickly looked away, back at the cool, calm ceiling. Her eyes traced the boring white tiles for the thousandth time; she had learned that focusing on them helped take her mind off the creeping threat of throwing up.

Ugh! I can't take this! Becca slid her hands beneath her and moved into a sitting position. The quick movement made her head spin, and the all too familiar queasiness came back. She pulled her knees to her chest and took deep, slow breaths. Her stomach bubbled and she glanced down at the bucket. Reaching out, her hand was halfway down before she changed her mind.

NO! Not again. I am not getting sick again!

As this resolve blazed within her, she felt a surge of energy escape from her brain and blast down her arm. The unseen energy crossed her wrist and briefly pooled in her palm, then shot out straight at the bucket, knocking it viciously backward.

Becca stared dumbfounded as she watched the bucket roll away. It had all happened in a second, maybe half a second. But it had happened.

What was that?

She lifted her hand and looked at it in the dim light. It looked the same, nothing unusual, but what…? Then she noticed something—her head felt better. That ringing, skull-splitting pain that had been festering for so long had eased a little, like she had let some air out of a near-bursting balloon.

Whatever that was, it helped.

Glancing down at her sheets, Becca decided to try something. She moved her hand above her sheets and held it flat, her palm downward.

Move, she thought.

Nothing happened.

Come on! Move.

Still nothing.

Becca grunted and stared around her. Maybe her sheets were too close. Across the aisle was another soldier's bed. This soldier was mumbling softly, but Becca couldn't understand anything she was saying. Next to her bed was a half-full glass of water. Glancing around the room first, Becca lifted her hand and tried again.

Okay, glass, move.

The glass stood still.

Come on, move... COME ON!

Becca gasped. The glass, which moments before had been resting on the wooden side table, was now hovering an inch above the surface. She held her hand as still as she could. Quickly glancing around again, she decided to try something else.

Okay, okay. I got this.

Slowly, Becca raised her shaking hand, and as she did the glass moved with it. Floating silently through the air, the glass moved upward and hovered over the sleeping soldier. Becca glanced at the window above the soldier's bed and raised the water glass higher. It edged upward, and the light from the moon illuminated its contents.

Becca smiled.

There's no way this is real. Maybe I've started hallucinating.

But even as she had this thought, she knew she wasn't hallucinating. Cautiously, she lowered her hand to place the glass back down. The glass, however, came down faster than she had anticipated and slammed onto the table with a crash. The glass shattered and water poured over the side of the table where it pooled on the floor and glittered in the moonlight. Becca held her breath, waiting for someone to move... but no one did. The soldiers continued to moan in their troubled sleep, and there was no movement from the nurse. Relieved, Becca let out her breath and looked around the room.

Tissues. She would move the stack of tissues next. Concentrating, she aimed both hands at them. They didn't move. She grunted and sat up straighter in her bed, focusing solely and completely on moving them. For a few more moments, nothing happened, then the stack slowly floated off the table. A wide grin broke over Becca's face. Sweating slightly from the strain, she swished her right hand down in a reverse arc, which moved half the stack down and over. It worked! Becca decided to experiment a little more.

With every move of her hands, she controlled the movements of the tissues. She moved them left and right, spun them in circles, and even made them race each other around the nearest soldier's bed. Becca grinned broadly; the intense pounding in her head was gone. Panting slightly from the effort it took to keep the tissues in the air, she raised them higher and prepared to launch them across the room when a muffled thud echoed from behind her.

Becca froze, her heart pounding. A squeak of rusty hinges told her the nurse's door was opening. She flung herself back down and drew her sheets over her right as the nurse came out of her office. The tissues, which had been floating ten feet off the ground, slowly drifted down and settled on top of a whimpering soldier.

Becca heard the nurse's steps hesitate, but apparently seeing nothing, she went on with checking her patients. As the nurse flitted from bed to bed Becca did her best to slow her breathing to the steady rhythm of sleep; a difficult task, as her heart was beating as though she had just finished a run with a drill sergeant. She waited for the nurse to come over, hoping that she wouldn't check her pulse.

A few silent minutes passed, then Becca heard a "What's this?" from the nurse.

The tissues!

She held her breath, but the nurse didn't seem very suspicious.

I guess she's seen weirder.

Becca kept waiting, and it wasn't long before she could feel the shadow of the nurse loom over her. Focusing on her breathing, she tried to seem relaxed. The nurse bent down and righted Becca's bucket with a click of her tongue. She felt Becca's forehead, hovered for another moment, then moved on.

Becca's slightly tensed muscles relaxed under her blankets as she listened to the nurse retreating. Hopefully she would leave soon, and she could get back to playing with this new... power-thing.

"AHHHHHH!"

Becca jumped as a soldier at the end of the room began screaming at the top of his lungs and thrashing in his bed. The nurse whipped around and sprinted over to him calling his name, trying to get him to calm down. Becca, along with a few others, raised themselves to get a look at the scene before lying back down.

I guess that's it for tonight, she thought, then closed her eyes and rolled over. Her mind kept spinning, trying to figure out what had just happened. It was then that she fully registered that the searing in her head was completely gone, and the tumbling of her stomach with it. Becca hid a smile in her pillow and, finally relieved of her pain, drifted off into a deep sleep.

***

The next day, things got a lot better for Becca. Whatever had happened last night had fixed everything. The headache was gone, and by now every other sign of illness had faded away too.

When the nurse came to check her in the morning, she couldn't believe what she was seeing. After she had taken a good look at Becca, she called the doctor over.

Becca didn't want to be looked at anymore, but figured that if he declared her better too, there would be fewer checkups in her future. Dr. Rosner looked her over carefully and asked her how she was feeling. By the time he had completed his examination, he had to agree with the nurse—all of Becca's symptoms were gone. Unfortunately, she was still very weak, so he told her that she had to stay in bed and rest for another week.

Another whole week in the hospital was not appealing. She wanted to get back out there and train with everyone else and to learn what was going on, but there was no arguing with Dr. Rosner. So, she stayed put and followed orders. Her only hope was that this week would go by faster than the past month had.

Becca spent the rest of the day studying the maps the others had brought her and eating everything that was put in front of her. If she was to get better, she was going to do it quickly. As the hours ticked by Becca found herself checking the clock frequently, waiting for Neal to come visit. She knew he was anxious for her to get better, and now that she finally was she couldn't wait to see his face. But what she really wanted to talk to him about was last night. Maybe he could help her understand what had happened.

Finally, at half past eight, the door opened to Becca's right and she looked up to see Neal strolling over to her. She smiled and waved him over. He looked at her curiously, clearly noticing that something had changed. Becca's smile widened; it made her happy that he could tell.

"Neal! I'm better! No headache, no puking, no chills!"

He grinned at her. "Excellent!" he said. "So are they letting you out?"

"No, not yet. Doc said I'm still too weak, he wants me strengthen up a bit, so I have to stay here for another week."

"Oh," he said, looking disappointed. "Well, at least the pain is gone."

"Yeah, and trust me, I don't miss it! Having a headache that lasts for a month is the worst kind of torture."

Neal's brow creased.

"Don't worry," Becca said. "I'm fine now. Plus, it's not like there's anything you could have done."

Neal opened his mouth to say something.

"Don't say you should have gotten me off the hill sooner *again*," Becca said, raising her hand to stop him. "It's *not* your fault. Anyway, there's something I wanted to talk to you about!" She patted the end of her bed. "Sit down."

Neal obliged, looking curiously at her. Sitting forward, she crossed her legs and looked at him excitedly. She was about to burst with the news, but she also didn't want to freak him out.

"Becca? What is with you? It's like you were just told the war is over," Neal said.

"Neal, you won't believe this. Okay, it's going to sound a bit crazy. Actually, it might sound very crazy, but I swear it's the truth. I haven't had a chance to do it since last night, not with everything going on, but—"

This time Neal put his hand up. "Becca, what on earth are you talking about? What did you do last night?"

"Sorry, sorry, I'm just…" She took a deep breath and looked around. Neal looked too. Everyone was busy, no one was watching them. Not even the nurse.

"Okay, Neal…" She looked at him again, her eyes huge.

"What? Just tell me already!"

"I moved stuff last night," she whispered.

Neal blinked. "You moved stuff? Becca, come on, I thought you said you had something to tell me."

"No, no, I mean it!" she hissed. "Neal, I made things move without touching them. I stayed right here, and they moved around. Anywhere I wanted them to. I made a glass of water float above her over there, and some tissues fly around over there. Wherever I wanted! It was the strangest thing. I know you probably don't believe me.

Actually, I'm not sure I believe it myself. I mean, like I said, I haven't had the chance to do it again since last night, but I'm pretty sure I wasn't dreaming. Look, I know it's crazy, but—"

"I believe you," Neal muttered, gazing off into the window behind Becca.

She stared at him. *Well, that was a lot easier than I thought it would be.* "What?"

"I believe you," Neal repeated, looking into her eyes this time.

Blinking, Becca shook her head. "Okay then... Wait. Why?"

Neal hesitated, then leaned closer to make sure they couldn't be heard. "Because I think I saw you do it."

"When?" She was leaning forward too.

"Well, I think I saw it a couple of times actually," Neal said, ruffling his hair distractedly. "Ever since the lightning. I thought I was imagining it at first, but then you made a pen in Sergeant Nelson's room spin, and while you've been here, things would float a bit after you touched them."

"Spin... and float?"

"Yeah, the pen just hovered off the ground and spun," Neal said, holding up his fingers to show what he meant.

Becca nodded and they sat in silence for a moment, not sure what to make of the situation. Now that she had said it out loud, Becca was

114

realizing how strange this was. She began to wonder if it was going to be permanent. Or what if whatever was happening last night was over now? Her headache was gone, after all… Or what if there was something else she could do, and she just didn't know it yet?

"It makes the pain in my head go away," she finally said.

Neal raised his eyebrows.

"Moving things. Every time I did it last night, the pain… seeped out. That's why I'm better now. Do you… do you think this is because of the lightning?"

Neal hesitated. "Maybe," he said. "I mean, those *were* weird lights… Can you still do it then? Move stuff?"

"I think so."

Becca sat back and pushed the bed sheets toward Neal. Then, with a quick look around again, she focused all her thoughts on the sheets. Slowly, quietly, they began sliding toward her. Neal watched in amazement. Then, as she placed her hand back down, the sheets stopped. Becca looked back up at Neal, her eyes shining once again. "Still got it." She grinned.

Neal shook his head. "This can't be real."

"I know. But I'm pretty sure it is."

The two of them fell into silence again. Neal dangled his feet over the edge of the bed and watched some patients laughing together at the end of the ward. Becca followed suit, thinking about what to do next. All of it seemed so surreal. Moving things without having to touch them? She had never heard of anything like this before.

"Should we tell Sarge?" she asked.

Neal was quiet for a moment, then shook his head. "No. At least, not yet."

"Why not?"

"You know Sarge. He'll think it was an enemy tactic or something. He'll freak out."

"Should he?" Becca said quietly.

Neal turned, his eyes flicking over her suddenly nervous face. "What?"

"Freak out. I mean, is this bad? What if those lights *were* the work of the Lossians? Maybe they've infused me with something?"

He shook his head. "I don't think so. The lights didn't come from their direction. How could they have aimed at us from the south? We're practically as far from the front as possible. There's no way. No, this was something else."

It was Becca's turn to nod. "So, now what?"

Neal stared out of the window on the opposite wall. "I don't know."

Chapter Nine

The rest of the week passed by a little too slowly for Becca's taste. The others came to visit her as well, as they wanted to keep her updated on their training—plus, Neal had told them the good news of her recovery. They were all excited for her to come back, but none of them were more excited than she was. She was sick of staying in bed, and ready to run through some mud or climb up a hill.

At night, when she was sure that the nurse was asleep and none of the other soldiers in the ward were stirring, she would get up and practice her new ability. It seemed the more she exercised it, the easier it became.

She continued moving tissues at first. They were light, and easy enough to control, but as she moved on to heavier objects, she found them harder to manipulate. The strain of moving these objects caused her to sweat heavily and exhausted her quickly. After struggling for half an hour to move a chair across the room one night, Becca collapsed into a deep sleep on the floor next to her bed, and was woken up the next day by the nurse lifting her up.

She tried again the next night, and was able to move the chair down a few rows after an hour of effort. Sticky with sweat, she stood up and walked into the aisle between the beds. She turned around and faced her hospital bed. Focusing with every ounce of energy she had, Becca extended her hands and tried to lift her bed. Nothing happened.

Huffing with exasperation, she wiped the sweat from her forehead and tried again. Still nothing. For the next three hours, she continued her efforts, but no matter how hard she tried she couldn't do it. Finally, she gave in to her exhaustion and shuffled over to her bed, where she collapsed and fell asleep immediately.

Three more days passed, and finally the day came when Becca could leave the hospital. The night before, the nurse had given her permission to leave first thing in the morning, so as soon as she woke up she made straight for the girls' dormitory.

Becca trotted down the empty halls, excited to be out of the hospital wing for the first time in over a month. Even the sight of the classrooms gave her a thrill. She grinned and hurried on.

Just as the sun had begun to pull itself over the horizon, she arrived at the dormitory. She strolled past the rows of bunks and made her way to her own. She then bent down, opened her chest, and pulled out one of her uniforms. Smiling, she undressed and put on her uniform once again. It was good to be back. With a quick glance around, she extended her hand toward the chest, which then closed itself. Becca's smiled widened.

Oh, yes. It's good to be back.

The loud ringing of the morning bell filled the air, and suddenly the still room around her hopped to life. The girls quickly got ready, mumbling tired but happy greetings at Becca. Soon everyone filed out of the room, heading directly for training.

Lizzy and Ruth slid into line next to Becca.

"How are you feeling?" Ruth whispered.

"Much better! I can't wait to get started! I don't think I could have stayed in that hospital bed for another day."

"Well, it's good to have you back," said Lizzy. "Now we can kick some other regiment butt. We're doing one of the practice drills today."

"At least she hopes we are," said Ruth.

Becca laughed, a new spring in her step. The group made their way down the hallway and turned left, where they met up with the boys. Neal, Matt, and Nick waved tiredly at the girls, giving an extra nod of greeting to Becca as they shuffled along. Together they went through the hallways down to the gym but, instead of lining up there, were ordered to go outside; so they walked straight through the rear gym doors and then the gates and out into the fields. Here, they were greeted by their drill sergeants with shouts to pick up the pace. Running now, the various regiments filed into their ready positions, where they were ordered to stop.

"Attention!" shouted a particularly loud drill sergeant.

Everyone on the field shifted and stood straighter, eyes forward. The drill sergeants went up to their assigned regiments, and the fun began. Starting with a brisk run around the 160 yards of field, they then did 200 jumping jacks, 80 quick push-ups, and 30 twenty-second sprints. Finally, the head drill sergeant blew a loud whistle and everyone stood at attention again. The sun, which had only just completed rising above the horizon when they had started, was now high in the sky sending down waves of heat. The soldiers breathed heavily as they awaited further commands, sweat streaming down their faces. The head drill sergeant walked in front of them and made his way to a lifted platform.

"Alright, soldiers, listen up!" he shouted at them. "Now that we've finished our light warm-up, we will move on to drilling one of our fighting scenarios today. Your regiments will be paired off and then your drill sergeants will give you instructions. You will follow their instructions and work together to complete your goal. Once you hear three loud blasts from my whistle, time is up. Then you lucky dogs will have the rest of the day off. You don't deserve it, but you get it. Work your sorry butts hard, and maybe, just maybe, I'll call the whistle early. That is all."

With that, he stepped down from the platform and the other drill sergeants addressed their individual regiments. Becca was standing next to Neal, and she gave him an excited look. Neal rolled his eyes.

Their regiment was paired off with Regiment 439 and told that they were to gather their gear and go out to the rubble of the training grounds. This area had been divided up, and each pair of regiments had to accomplish their task within their section. Each regiment's mission was to get to the end of their opponent's zone, where they would retrieve the "classified information" and then make it back without being seen. If caught, they would have to fight their way out.

Regiment 427 was assigned paint guns with yellow paint, while Regiment 439 was given red. If hit, they were dead. Their job was to complete the mission while losing as few team members as possible. Not an easy task, as their sections were small and close together. They would really have to work as a team and be stealthy in order to pull this off.

Becca bounced on her toes, and Neal shook his head in amused exasperation. "You've got issues," he whispered as he leaned past her to grab a paint gun and yellow paint pellets from the storage cabinet.

She made a face in reply, then turned and ran back out to join the others.

A loud whistle sounded out, and everyone stood at attention. "Alright soldiers, to your areas!" came the order from somewhere behind them, and they all moved. This training ground was all rubble, filled with destroyed bits of buildings and scattered with old train carts and ditches. It was very random, assembled to look like a part of a battlefield. Dispersed throughout the grounds were four large trees. Built into these were flat platforms that the drill sergeants and sometimes head sergeants stood on to watch the progress.

The entire training area had been divided into three long sections that were further divided into two zones—one for each opponent. Neal and Becca slid into line as their regiment passed through the first mess of rubble and stone, making their way deeper into their zone. The thirty members of their regiment soon pooled together in between a dilapidated building and a particularly large stone. Then they all looked at each other for what to do next.

"Well," one soldier finally said, "we should probably decide who is going to lead us."

Everyone nodded in agreement, but no one volunteered. When they lost these tactical exercises, the leader always had to do more push-ups than the rest of the team. They all looked at one another, but still no one spoke.

Neal sighed. "Fine, I'll do it."

Everyone nodded.

"Okay then," Neal started. "We should probably divide into groups, maybe three groups of ten? Then we should move in waves into the enemy zone, that way we can't all get shot down...Um, obviously take out any enemy you see... Everyone is responsible for their own group..." Neal glanced around, seemingly trying to think of what else to say, but meeting unhelpfully blank faces. "So, sound good?" he said.

Becca and the rest nodded in agreement.

"Great, then, let's get to it."

With mutters of excitement all around, the regiment broke off into groups.

Neal, Becca, Matt, Ruth, Lizzy, and Nick all stayed in a group with Dave, Lacy, and two other soldiers named Benson and Clouts. Together their group moved to the front to be the first wave. Usually, whoever was the leader also led the offensive. Nodding at the second group as they left them behind, their group moved cautiously forward to the edge of their zone.

A loud whistle blast sounded from one of the tree posts. It was time to start.

Neal glanced at his group and nodded. The ten broke off into three smaller teams—Becca joining with Neal, Ruth, and Matt—and headed in different directions. Slowly, quietly, they moved their way forward and to the left, on high alert for their enemies. They came to a particularly high bit of rock and Neal turned and nodded at Ruth.

Ruth gave Neal a thumbs-up, then slung her gun onto her back, climbed up to the top of the rock, and ducked behind a large bump in the front. From there she had a good view of the land in front of them and a good shot at anyone who might be coming. Ruth gave Neal a quick wave and pulled her gun back out.

Neal nodded. "Okay," he said to Becca and Matt. "She's got us covered, let's go."

Becca was thrilled as she set off after Neal and Matt. This was her favorite drill; it felt so real. It was very quiet, and the mix of rubble and broken buildings had an eerily strong effect on their minds.

Becca could feel the hairs on the back of her neck tingle as they slowly made their way through. So far, they had run into no one. A shot sounded off somewhere far to their right. They stopped and listened. This shot was quickly followed by more, along with shouted orders and the echoes of running feet.

Neal looked back at Becca and Matt, who gave nods. He then waved them forward, keeping to the walls. They spotted an overturned and beaten-up train cart and moved carefully towards it. Glancing around first, they sprinted up and held their backs against it. Becca raised her eyebrows at Neal and gestured to the corner of the cart. He nodded in reply and led the way there.

Becca went low and followed Neal closely. He was just about to poke his head around a corner when a shot rang out from above them, quickly followed by a thud and a disappointed grunt nearby. Becca jumped up and around him in a flash. Someone from the other regiment stood there with a yellow paint splatter dead on his chest. Ruth had got him in one clean shot, but behind him were two more soldiers. Neal and Becca quickly took shots before ducking back around the corner.

Neal's shot had hit its mark, but Becca's had missed. One left. Neal looked over his shoulder at Matt.

"The other side," he whispered.

Matt nodded and moved to the far end, while Neal got ready to move around his corner again. Becca went to the center and made to back up in a few quick steps in case their opponent had climbed to the top.

"Now!" Neal shouted.

The three of them pounced, and with a ring of shots both Matt and the other soldier were splattered with paint.

"Ah, sorry guys," Matt said.

"Don't worry about it," Neal replied. "Come on, Becca!"

"Coming! Later, dead boy!" Becca said to Matt.

Matt smiled and turned to head back out to the field. Becca gave a quick wave to Ruth in thanks, then followed Neal further into the hostile zone. More shots rang out from other parts of the training ground as they crept onward, sending chills up Becca's back. Then the sound of feet on gravel came from somewhere nearby, and they froze in their tracks. Becca glanced around them and saw what used to be an old shed.

"Quick, in here," she said, grabbing Neal by the arm.

They ran to the shed and ducked into the darker corners. Exercise or not, this drill got their blood pumping, and the two had to do their best to slow their breathing.

125

"Come on, I thought I heard something," came a voice.

Becca looked around and noticed that two of the boards next to her had separated just enough to see through. She shifted her position and peered through the gap in the wall. Two soldiers were coming towards them, guns pointed toward the shed. Becca held up two fingers, and Neal nodded in response.

She looked through the gap again and noticed a loose rock sitting right above where the two soldiers were walking. She grinned.

It's too easy.

Raising her hand, she focused on the rock, trying to hoist it from its resting place. If she could get it just right and make it land close enough to the soldiers to scare them, then they could pounce. Silently, she strained to lift the rock. Sweat started to gather on her forehead. It looked lighter than her hospital bed, so she could do this.

Come on, come on!

The rock started to move.

Yes!

Suppressing a grunt, Becca forced the rock up a little further.

In her periphery she noticed Neal lean forward and peek through another hole in the wall. "Becca, no!" he whispered a second later.

126

But she ignored him. She focused harder and edged the rock forward. Neal lunged at her and yanked her hand down. Her focus was broken, and the rock rolled back into its original position on the ledge she had been trying to move it from.

Becca jerked her arm away. "What are you doing?"

"Are you crazy, what if somebody sees you?!" he hissed.

"I had that! I was just going to scare them!"

"Becca, what if you missed? What if a drill sergeant saw you doing that?"

"Come on, I—"

"Hello there," interrupted a deep voice.

The two of them spun around only to be greeted with the end of a barrel. A second later there were two cracks, and they had red paint splattered over the front of their uniforms. Neal and Becca sighed.

The soldier laughed. "Honestly," he said. "You two really need to learn to be quieter." With that he shouldered his gun and jogged away from the shed.

"Nice going!" said Becca. "Now we're out, and we're probably going to lose. If you had just let me move the rock I could have distracted them, and we would still be in right now."

Neal shook his head. "Becca, you could have hurt them! You could have been caught! Do you *want* to get caught? Because if you do, by all means throw some rocks around. I won't stop Sergeant Nelson or the doctor when they decide to do experimental tests on you."

Becca felt heat creep up her face as she led the way out of the shed. "Do you actually think they would have seen that? One rock, Neal, it was one rock!"

Neal gave a low grumble as he pushed past her. "Whatever, Becca, let's just get out and see how everyone else is doing."

The two of them said nothing more as they trudged back towards the open field. They passed a few more soldiers who were in the exercise, but with a quick raise of their hands they showed that they were out and kept moving. Eventually, they made it past the last bit of rocks and walked over to their other fallen teammates. Matt and Lizzy were sitting with about nine more members.

"You guys too, huh?" Matt greeted them.

"Yeah, well, Neal gave away our location," Becca sighed.

"No, that was definitely you," Neal snapped back.

Becca turned to him, her eyes flashing. "You know what—?"

"Hey, hey!" Matt said, standing up and placing himself between the two. "It's just an exercise, guys, calm down."

Becca continued to glare at Neal, who returned the look. Matt stayed between them until he was sure they wouldn't attack each other, then sat down. Neal joined him on the grass, but Becca walked farther away and sat down alone. Lizzy gave the boys a nervous glance, then went over to sit next to her.

"So, who else is out?" Becca asked Lizzy.

"Well, Regiment 436 is completely out," Lizzy said. "Four-thirty-two is as well. So, at least we can't be dead last. Plus, about half of our team is still in there, right?"

Becca nodded. "Ruth's in there," she said. "They'll never get her."

Lizzy grinned. "I've never met someone who can move so quietly."

"Not to mention she's a perfect shot."

"Yeah. As long as she's in, we still have a chance at winning this."

"And if it wasn't for loudmouth over there, we'd still be in there too," Becca muttered, scowling at Neal's back.

"Cut him some slack, Bec," Lizzy said. "I'm sure he's just excited you're back. It's throwing him off his game."

Becca grunted, but said nothing else. They all sat in silence, waiting for the next paint-stained person to walk out of the training ground.

For twenty more minutes the group waited and watched as soldiers from their own team and the others slowly drifted back out on the field. The sounds from within could still be heard, but they came much less frequently now. Instead, their ears became filled with the increasing roars of their empty stomachs. Time seemed to have slowed down and sweat trickled uncomfortably down their backs as the blazing sun bore down on them. Many were beginning to care much less about who won, so long as someone did soon. The soldiers on the grass kept their eyes on the tree posts, watching for signs from the drill sergeants, but so far there had been nothing.

Another ten minutes went by and the tired, hungry soldiers who were now sprawled all over the grass finally heard three loud whistle blows from the sergeants. A cheer went up and everyone shuffled to their feet to see who the winners were. It had come down to Regiments 430 and 427. Ruth and Nick were the only ones from Regiment 427 who hadn't come out yet; Becca crossed her fingers, hoping that they would be the ones without the paint stains.

Two painfully slow minutes went by then finally the figures of Ruth and Nick emerged, paint free. Becca cheered along with the rest, noticing that Neal cheered the loudest—he was probably relieved he didn't have to do fifty extra push-ups. Running forward, they all gave Ruth and Nick loud thumping hugs before dropping off their guns and making their way back inside for lunch.

As they walked Becca stole a glance at Neal, but he refused to meet her eye. She huffed and pushed past him to join Lizzy and Ruth. Glancing over her shoulder at the training area, Becca noticed Sergeant Nelson among the drill sergeants on a platform. As she watched he leaned over and said something to one of the other drill sergeants, and if she was not mistaken, they were both looking right at Neal. Again, she glanced at Neal, but he didn't seem to notice. Shrugging, Becca turned her thoughts to the lunch menu.

Chapter Ten

Within fifteen minutes all the regiments were changed, in the dining hall, and scarfing down late lunches. Exhausted and starving, the thought consuming everyone's minds was how much food they could choke down. Neal, Becca, and the others were crowded around Nick and Ruth listening eagerly between bites to hear how they had won the practice drill.

"Well," Nick said. "Ruth ran into me after Dave and Clouts had been caught. She had seen them get hit, and decided to go down. Then we moved forward and she found another high spot to keep an eye out on. Honestly, I wasn't sure how many were left of the other team, were you, Ruth?"

She shrugged. "I had a general idea, but I couldn't be sure."

"Of course you did. So, apparently Ruth knew how many were left and didn't tell me," Nick continued as the others laughed. "Well anyway, we decided that I should just keep pushing through, hoping we could get to the end without getting shot. Ruth here stayed on the perch we found and

132

to be honest I really relied on her to take down anyone near me. I would hear a shot—bang!—then come up to a corner and slowly edge around it, only to see the guy splattered in paint. Ruth took down everyone in my way, and before long I had made it to the other side, and there was only one guy left, so—"

"So he and Nick dueled it out, and Nick won," Ruth finished.

The others cheered and slapped Ruth and Nick on the back. Ruth smiled embarrassedly, but Nick waved at them to keep the praise coming.

"Well, I'm glad Nick was there, because I couldn't have done it on my own," Ruth said.

"Oh shut up," Lizzy said. "You have the best ears, Ruth. You would have heard anyone coming before they even knew you were in range."

The others agreed heartily with Lizzy and pressed Ruth for more details. Only half listening at this point, Neal snuck a glance at Becca, who was currently doing everything she could to avoid his gaze.

She's so frustrating! Neal squeezed his sandwich so hard the meat slipped out, and he aggressively shoved it back between the slices of bread. *She's been back for what, half a day, and she's already pushing the limits? She shouldn't be so reckless with her new ability. If someone had seen her...*

He didn't want to think about that. He scowled as he took a bite of his sandwich and tried to focus on what Ruth was saying instead.

Ten minutes later everyone had finished eating. After that they all scattered in one direction or another to enjoy the rest of their day off. Matt said he was off to study some medical books, and Ruth went with to keep him company. Lizzy had some maps she wanted to study up on, and Nick mumbled something about a nap and shuffled off. That left Neal and Becca standing alone. He looked over at her; she was still avoiding eye contact.

With a shrug Neal started off down the hallway, thinking that maybe he'd listen to the radio in the rec room. He had barely made it two steps, however, before he felt Becca's hand on his arm. He looked over his shoulder.

"Look," she said. "I just wanted to say sorry. What I did, it was probably a bit stupid."

Neal raised his eyebrows at her. "Yeah, it was stupid." He resumed walking down the hall.

"Wait!" Becca called after him. "Neal, wait!"

He stopped and turned around.

"Come on, I said I was sorry, didn't I?"

"Yeah, but Bec, I don't think you understand, if you expose to everyone what you can do—"

"What?" Becca snapped. "What? I mean honestly, what's the worst that can happen if people find out about this?"

Neal blinked. "What's the worst that could happen?" he shouted back. "Becca, look, if Sergeant Nelson or any of the others learned that those lights

134

did something to you, they'll go ballistic. They're already freaked out by everything going on in the front. There's a lot they don't understand, and if they get wind about you they'll try to figure out if you're some sort of danger, or they'll try to turn you into some sort of weapon, or they'll—" Neal stopped at his next thought.

"What?" Becca demanded.

"Lock you up…" he muttered, keeping his eyes firmly focused on the ground.

"They'll lock me up?" She sounded skeptical.

"Yeah, maybe!" he said defiantly. "And if they do I wouldn't be able to… I mean, we wouldn't… well, you wouldn't be able to fight," he finished quickly, looking anywhere but at Becca.

He could feel her stare and the heat rising up the back of his neck. Becca said nothing, and they stood there in silence for the longest fifteen seconds Neal could remember.

"Anyway," he said, clearing his throat. "I should probably—"

"Yeah," said Becca. "I think I'm going to rest, you know… still a bit weak."

Neal watched her as she walked away. Then, muttering to himself, he continued walking toward the rec room.

Why did I say that? It was stupid… But she was being reckless, and it was only her first day back. It would have been so easy for her to be caught, and then taken away.

Doesn't she realize that? Doesn't she care that she could be taken away from me... Neal shook his head. *Us. Doesn't she care that she could be taken away from all of us?*

Clearing his throat again anxiously, Neal turned down another hallway and approached the door to the rec room. It was crowded with exhausted soldiers lounging about. He shuffled his way through the maze of chairs and feet and found an open chair alone in a corner. With a sigh, he flopped down, leaned back, and closed his eyes. The last few weeks had worn him down, and now that he wasn't flooded with worry about Becca's health, his exhaustion was catching up with him.

Although, if she carried on the way she did today, he was going to have a lot more to worry about. Clearly, she was excited about this new ability and would want to take every chance to test it and see what she could do, but he couldn't shake the feeling that revealing it would land her in a lot of trouble. Neal ran his hand through his hair. He still had no idea what to make of those lights, or this new ability of Becca's.

Sure, he had learned more of the legends of the strong warriors who had helped form and found their Nation, but nothing about them having beyond normal human powers. Yet, here Becca was with the flummoxing ability to move things through the air without touching them. Neal sat up and rubbed his eyes, then stared blankly around the room. It had to have been those lights that had done this to her, whatever they were. There was no other thing that could have caused this. Sighing again, he was just thinking that maybe he should go back to researching the lights when he was startled back to the present moment.

"Hey, *hey*!" bellowed an older soldier named Lott over the hubbub of the rec room. "Shut up, everyone! Shut up for a moment."

His booming voice silenced everyone immediately, and they all stared at the radio as they listened to the latest report.

"Powerful new weapons have overcome our troops at the front. We have been pushed back past the High Rise River and into the surrounding villages. The inhabitants of the villages fled as the battle raged towards them, but unfortunately we do not know how many have escaped. Our forces were able to hold them at bay just before the Blackened Hills, making this the farthest the Lossian Nation has pushed into our territories throughout this long war. Members of the Edscaftian Council—"

No one was listening anymore; an outcry had erupted in the rec room. Neal sat back, stunned. This was a heavy blow for their military. The High Rise River had always acted as a sort of mental safety net. The Edscaftian troops had always maintained the idea that as long as the High Rise River was behind them, then they were still making headway into the Lossian Nation. Now they had lost their ground, and from the sound of things it hadn't been much of a fight.

Not a minute passed before a piercing ringing blasted throughout the camp. A tingle went up Neal's spine and he stood up abruptly. Everyone in the rec room froze as one wave of the alarm, then another met their ears. Then they all moved at once. Every soldier in the room filed into the hall and moved quickly toward the front entrance. It was the dreaded sound of their emergency signal, and protocol was to meet in the courtyard to await orders.

The crowded hallways echoed with the pounding of boots. Neal kept his eyes peeled for Becca and the others as he moved along. He followed the pack, thumping down the stairs and into the next hallway. As he rounded a corner, he saw Becca. She had spotted him as well, and shouldered her way over.

"Neal, what's going on?"

"I'm not sure," he replied. "But did you hear about what's happened at the front?"

"No, I was in the dorm when the alarm went off. What happened?"

Neal didn't reply; he had just spotted Matt and Ruth. Grabbing Becca's arm, he pulled her through the thick mass of soldiers. They squeezed past two particularly large guys to join Matt and Ruth.

"Neal, Becca!" Matt said. "Do you know what's going on?"

"No, but I doubt it's good," Neal replied.

They arrived at the main doors, and what met their eyes sent shivers up Neal's spine. Large military trucks were pouring through the gates and into their courtyard. Neal and the others followed the rest of the soldiers down the steps and shuffled into lines according to their regiments, their footsteps echoing coldly off the stone walls. With amazing speed all the regiments were outside and standing at attention. Despite the sense of panic now rising in Neal's chest, he couldn't help but be impressed. The entire camp had been cleared in three minutes flat.

They all stood silently, struggling to slow their panting breaths as they watched truck after truck pass through the gate. Neal noted that besides the drivers, the trucks were empty. Another flicker of panic coursed through him as he began to understand what was going on. Neal shot a glance at Becca, who returned it nervously.

From behind them, Sergeant Nelson came down the steps. He passed through their lines and went straight to the truck in the front. Someone stepped out from the passenger seat. The five stripes down the left arm of his uniform told them that this was a general. His large square jaw matched his square and straight uniform. His sharp blue eyes scanned the soldiers and came to rest on Sergeant Nelson.

"General Hopps." Sergeant Nelson saluted.

"Sergeant." The general saluted back, his deep voice resounding through the courtyard. "Glad to see you got our message in time."

"Yes, sir. They're all here, and I can personally vouch for every regiment. They are all ready for transport and deployment per your discretion."

"Excellent. We will go to your office to discuss this. Tell all of your troops to be ready at a moment's notice," he growled.

"Yes, sir," Sergeant Nelson said. He then spun on his heel and relayed the command to the soldiers before him.

This was hardly necessary, as everyone in the courtyard had heard what General Hopps had said. However, they all replied with a salute and stood at attention as the general and the sergeant walked into the compound. The moment the two superiors were gone, the soldiers followed in a rushed silence.

Neal could feel his heart pounding somewhere near his throat. *Transport and deployment?* He leaned over and whispered to Becca. "The radio report just said that we have been pushed past the High Rise River and into the Blackened Hills. We must be on the move because of that."

"What?!" she said. "How far into the hills have we been pushed?"

"Far enough to evacuate more of the nearby villages."

Becca's eyes widened and Neal knew she understood. They were being moved up.

The soldiers broke off and flooded their respective dorms with a speed that came from years of training and drilling. They packed their few belongings into their bags, threw them over their shoulders, and headed to the weapons room, where each grabbed a gun. Then they made their way back to the courtyard.

Once outside, Neal filed into line between Becca and Matt and stood rigidly at attention. His mind was both reeling and completely numb. *Where are we going? Are we going to be sent out to the front tonight? Does Sergeant Nelson really think we're ready? Or is it out of sheer desperation that we're being pulled forward?*

No one moved for ten strained minutes. Then, the doors opened behind them with a bang, and General Hopps, Sergeant Nelson, and the head drill sergeant walked out in front of them. A collective breath was taken in, and it seemed as though no one let the air back out. They waited.

General Hopps whispered something to Sergeant Nelson, who nodded and saluted. Then the general got into his truck and began rifling through a large stack of papers. Sergeant Nelson turned to everyone.

"Alright," he barked. "Listen up. Things are moving fast, and due to some unforeseen changes on the front you're all being transferred today. Each regiment will divide themselves into two trucks that you will be assigned to, and you will head off to various camps. None of you are heading out to the field today, but some of you will be very close. Once you are at your new camp, you will be given your assignments." He paused and took a moment to look at all of them. "Good luck."

With that, Sergeant Nelson stepped back and let the head drill sergeant assign them to their trucks. There was a flurry of organized movement as each regiment split and filed onto their trucks. Following their group, Neal and the others headed to one parked on the far side of the courtyard and got in. Everyone was quiet, with only a few hushed whispers between them.

Their group sat very still as they watched the last few soldiers pile into their trucks. Then, Sergeant Nelson appeared at the back of their truck and scanned them. His eyes landed on Becca.

"Harraway," he barked.

Next to him, Neal could feel Becca tense up. "Yes, sir."

"Are you well enough to travel?"

"Yes, sir."

Sergeant Nelson nodded. "Good."

With that he turned and headed around the truck. They heard him talking to the driver, then the sound of the passenger door opening and slamming closed.

"He's coming with us?" Nick asked no one in particular.

"Sure, seems like it," Matt replied.

A minute later the truck started up and began rolling out. As one, Neal and the others turned their heads and looked out the back. They watched in silence as their train of trucks circled around the courtyard and out of the gate. They watched the buildings of Dune Hills slowly fade away, and with them, their sense of comfort. Dune

Hills had been their home for years now, and in the span of an hour, it wasn't anymore.

Sergeant Nelson said it, Neal thought. *Things are moving fast.*

Chapter Eleven

Three hours later and the trucks were still making their way through the Edscaftian Nation to their unknown destinations. Becca, Neal, and the others had exhausted the first hour and a half going over the events of that afternoon and every update they could remember hearing from the radio. They all had their own theories on where they were being taken, but in the end they knew these were just guesses; so after a while they gave up. Slowly, everyone succumbed to the soothing rumble of the road beneath the tires and the hum of the truck's engine. They all drifted off into a fitful sleep, only to be woken up again by their head jerking painfully off to the side.

The third time Becca jolted back to consciousness she decided to stay awake for a while, to avoid getting painful cramps in her neck. Shifting her position as quietly as possible, she stared out the back of the truck into the silky night. The sight was so peaceful. It was hard to accept that things could be so quiet when their lives had just been uprooted so suddenly.

Becca sighed and let her eyes glaze over as she thought about Dune Hills. They might not ever see it again, now that they were off to… wherever it was they were going. A sort of sadness crept in. It wasn't like Dune Hills was much of a home, but it was more of a home than the orphanage had been. As she pictured the camp, she was surprised to feel a deep ache tug at her heart.

Her bag fell over with a small thump, bringing her attention back to the truck. With a quick glance around to make sure everyone was still sleeping, Becca stretched her arm out and held her palm over the bag. She twitched her hand. The bag lifted itself up and settled upright against her leg. She gave a small smile.

Shifting her position, she began to bounce her leg and watched the dark landscape slip by. A few minutes later she felt a hand holding down her leg. She turned to see Neal yawning widely.

"You've seriously got to kick that habit," he mumbled.

Becca pushed his hand off of her leg. "It helps me think."

"About what?" he asked as he rubbed the back of his neck.

She shrugged. "I don't know. Just stuff."

Neal grunted and let his head fall back against the truck wall. They sat quietly listening to the rumbles of the truck when the sound of deep voices talking quietly drifted back to them.

145

"What do you think they're talking about?" Becca asked, looking at the wall separating Sergeant Nelson and the driver from the rest of them.

"Could be anything," Neal said. "Who knows what kind of information the general gave him earlier."

"Do you think they talked about the lights?"

He sat up a little straighter.

"I mean, do you think Sergeant Nelson is still worried that Lossi is the one behind them, and now the general knows?" she continued.

"It's possible," he said, giving her a worried look. "But they don't know about you, they only know you were sick for a long time."

"Well yeah," she said. "But what if they know more? What if the lights come back?"

He didn't say anything.

She turned her focus back to her bag and, stretching out her hand, lifted her water bottle out of the side pocket and into the air. He reached over and snatched the bottle with one hand, pushing her arm down with the other.

"Are you crazy?" he whispered. "What if the others see you?"

She scoffed and snatched the water bottle from his hands. "I'm just practicing. I think I can get better at this."

"Becca," he hissed. "You know that's dangerous. Didn't you just agree with me earlier today that it was dangerous?"

"No," she said, pulling her arm out of his grip. "No, I didn't." She crossed her arms and turned away from him.

"Becca—"

"Good night, Neal," she said. She closed her eyes and listened as he sighed and slowly shifted his position.

He just doesn't get it. She opened her eyes and looked over her shoulder at him. His eyes were closed as well, his mouth moving silently as he muttered to himself. She sniffed and turned around again, falling back to sleep moments later.

***

Time seemed to crawl by as the trucks wove their way through the Edscaftian Nation. Becca counted three small villages, one of the Nation's Great Lakes (she was pretty sure it was the Styrian Lake), and one city. The city of Mirfield. She knew that there were four major cities in the Edscaftian Nation, but she had never actually been to any of them before.

As they eased their way through the well-lit city streets, which were busy despite the very late hour, Becca couldn't help but stare. Tired- and worried-looking people bustled around each corner, many carrying large crates or bags stuffed with items she couldn't see. She wondered what everyone was up to. The caravan of military trucks turned down a narrow brick street and out into what appeared to be the center of the city, and Becca's jaw dropped.

Towering buildings surrounded the square like a window-covered fence, and inside this closed-in area were lines and lines of people. As she gazed around the square, Becca understood what was going on. The square was full of refugees from some of the outlying Edscaftian villages. They had flocked to the city looking for help.

Booths and stations had been set up around the square where other citizens were handing out supplies and giving directions to shelters. More people were pouring in from the streets and dropping off donations at booths backed by large crates.

Becca glanced over at Neal, who was looking out on the scene with a mixture of sadness and pride. She understood the feeling. Turning her gaze back out of the truck, she noticed that many people had stopped and were now staring at them. They were watching their military trucks roll through, their expressions mirroring Neal's.

The truck slowly eased out of the square and continued down the narrow streets lined with tall buildings. Becca watched every building pass with wide eyes, soaking it all in. Eventually, the trucks made it out of Mirfield and drove onward across the Nation.

***

At daybreak the trucks came to a stop. Somewhere along the road the caravan had split up, and now only the two trucks carrying Regiment 427 remained. The soldiers hopped out and stood at attention, waiting for Sergeant Nelson's orders. He informed them that this was only to be a quick stop to relieve themselves and refuel the trucks. When he dismissed them, they scattered, looking for private, secluded places.

Coming out of a dense thicket, Becca searched the nearby woods for a stream. She watched the ground carefully, searching for wet soil. When she spotted a darker patch of ground, she followed it deeper into the woods. Soon, she heard the rushing of nearby stream. Becca grinned, hurried over, and bent over it. She dipped her hands into the cold water in an effort to clean them, then reached into her pack and took out her bottle.

As she was filling it, Neal came up behind her. Silently he followed the same procedure. When he finished filling his bottle, he took a deep long drink, refilled it, and then stood up and stretched. Becca leaned back on her heels and watched him as he walked around. His knees were popping as he stretched them out.

"How much longer do you think we have?" she asked him.

Neal shrugged. "We're probably about halfway. The way the driver and Sergeant Nelson we're talking, it sounds like we still have a while to go."

Becca nodded, then stood up as well. She glanced around the clearing, then turned her focus to the rocks at her feet. She felt Neal watching her as she extended her right hand. A small stone rose off the ground, and she smiled. She lifted it higher and higher until it was at waist level.

"Becca," he said. "Don't."

"Why not?" She grinned at him. "There's no one here."

With a flick of her hand, the rock flung itself at the river and skipped across the water. It made twelve skips before sinking into the rumbling stream. Wanting to see if she could get a rock to skip farther, Becca lifted another into the air.

"Seriously, you can't just do that in the open. What if you get caught?" Neal said.

She turned and frowned at him, dropping the stone. "First of all, we're not in the open, we're in the middle of the woods. And second of all, what problem do you have with me being able to do this? There's nothing wrong with it. Why are you so worried I'll get caught?"

"Becca... look, I'll admit what you can do is amazing, but it's dangerous," Neal said.

"How?" She stood with her hands on her hips, glaring at him.

"Do I have to explain it again?" he growled. "We're soldiers, Bec. Not sticking to regulation is enough to get us in trouble. How do you think the Council will react when they find out one of their soldiers has the ability to move things with her mind?"

"They would probably love it! I can help with this. I can make a real difference in this war. Who knows how much I can lift and move?" Becca felt a shiver of excitement run through her. "I could get Sarlic Lossi back for killing my family. I could be the one who can finally help put a stop to this whole war!"

"And how are you going to do that?" he asked dryly.

She began pacing excitedly. "I don't know, I could just... help. If the Council knew of my power, they could put me where I could really use it. Maybe somehow help on a larger scale with taking down Sarlic's armies, or keeping them from crossing further into our lands, or protecting the cities!"

"Hold on, Becca, you don't—"

She didn't hear him; a wonderful idea had just occurred to her. "Or I could use my power to help lead our army over the border and finally face Sarlic. We could finally push back! I could make sure that our lands are never infiltrated by Sarlic's soldiers again. That Sarlic is put back where he belongs... that this war ends!"

She turned back to Neal, eager to share this amazing new possibility with him.

"Don't you see? *I'm* the answer to the problems our military has been facing! It was reported that our military was struggling, right?

Well, I can go out there and help them push back! If the Council—"

"No, Becca!" Neal stepped forward and grabbed her arms, trying to hold her still. "If the Council knew about your powers, the last thing they would do is send you to the front. They wouldn't trust you. They'd say that somehow Sarlic Lossi did this to you and that it's just another plot to take down the Edscaftian Nation. You saw how they reacted after the night you were struck!"

Becca felt a flush run up her face. She shook herself out of his grasp angrily and took a few steps back. "You don't know that. They could want me to help!"

Neal growled with exasperation and ran his hands through his hair. "Why don't you understand how dangerous this is?"

"Because it's not!" she fired back. "I wasn't hit by something from the Lossian Nation, there is *no way* they could reach all the way to the far south of our Nation. You said so yourself. Once the Council realizes this, they would want me to help!"

"Becca."

"No, Neal! Don't 'Becca' me." She crossed the distance between them and poked him hard in the chest. "You just don't want me to use my power because you're afraid I'm right! You're afraid the Council will think I'm the best chance at ending this war. You're afraid *I'll* be the one they ask to lead and *you'll* be left behind. You're afraid you won't be a hero like your brother. You've been afraid ever since Finn died, and now you're too afraid to actually fight. You act like this is what you want to do, but you're always the one who hesitates, who questions. And now, you're too afraid to let the Council know about my power!"

Neal blinked and stared down at Becca. She held his gaze, panting as though she had just run a mile. Then, with a huff of disgust, he turned away and began walking back to the truck.

"Neal!" she yelled after him. "You *know* that's the reason you don't want me to use this power! Why can't you just admit it?"

Neal stopped in his tracks, then whipped around to face her. Becca took a half step back. He had never looked at her like this before. He marched over to her, anger and hurt blazing in his eyes.

"Is that honestly what you think of me? That I'm a coward! Is that really why you think I don't want you to use your power?" he asked, his voice rising with every word. "Do you think glory and dying with honor are the reasons I joined this fight? My brother *died*, Becca! This isn't a joke. This isn't about finding glory on the field, or holding anyone back out of jealousy. This is war, with real consequences! This isn't about me and what I want, this is about what could happen, and what *will* happen if you're not careful!"

Becca glared back at him. Why didn't he see how stupid it was to worry about what the Council would think? She knew they would let her fight. She had just opened her mouth to tell him so when they heard another voice from their left.

"Hey guys…" Nick called uncertainly. "It's, uh, time to get back to the truck." He looked nervously between the two of them. "You two okay?"

Neal took a step back from Becca, still red in the face. "Fine," he said, walking over to Nick and giving him a pat on the shoulder. "We're fine."

"Okay…" Nick's gaze fell on Becca. He clearly didn't believe Neal, but followed him anyway.

Angry and frustrated tears stung Becca's eyes. She wiped them away hurriedly and stomped after the boys.

She grumbled all the way back to the truck. *Neal doesn't get it. He doesn't understand. I have to use this new power. It makes me feel… it makes me feel whole.* Becca wiped more tears off her face. Anyway, she knew she was right. She pushed a tree branch out of her path with unnecessary force. She could actually *do* something now that she had this power. More than she could do with a gun. Everyone knew she wasn't that great of a shot anyway.

When they arrived at the truck, Becca kept to the back of the group and watched as Neal grabbed his things and moved them between Nick and Lizzy at the other end of the bench. Choosing to be as far away as possible from her. Becca didn't care. Let him move if he wanted to. She sat down with her head high and didn't look at him. Instead, she smiled at Matt then stared determinedly out the back of the truck. With a rumble, the truck kicked back to life, and they continued their drive across the Nation.

Chapter Twelve

Their journey through the lands lasted the rest of day, with few stops. Becca sighed as she gazed out the back of the truck. Neal was still mad at her. She had been angry too for a while, but she figured he would have calmed down by the time the trucks took their next break. She had been wrong. Neal avoided her completely, then sat far away from her again. It was the same at their third stop, and now she was feeling guilty.

Maybe she had gone too far. She hadn't intended on calling him a coward, although part of her had always wondered why he wasn't as eager to fight as the rest of them. And she shouldn't have mentioned Finn. She knew better than to bring him up, or imply that his death was what made him great. That was stupid. She didn't really know why she had said it; she was just angry, and frustrated, and ready to do something more.

Becca stole a glance at Neal, who was still sitting between Ruth and Nick, talking quietly. He didn't look up at her. Becca noticed some other members of their regiment watching her. She quickly looked away, and with another sigh watched the landscape slip by in the warm sunset. They were passing through hilly country now, and the dim evening light made everything look more like a shadow than a solid object.

Beyond the hills, she knew there were more rivers, and beyond them forest. Villages and towns would be scattered in between. Becca wanted to go into the towns and learn about what was going on at the front, but the trucks wouldn't have time to stop. She still didn't know much about the retreat behind the High Rise River, and she wanted to know what had happened since. She wanted to know what Lossi was up to. She sighed again.

"What's with you?" asked Matt, who was sitting right next to her. "That's the third time you've sighed in the last two minutes."

"Sorry. It's just, Neal's mad at me."

"Yeah, I can tell."

Becca looked past Matt at Neal again. He had been glaring at her, but now avoided eye contact.

"What did you do?" Matt asked.

"Nothing, he's just being stupid," Becca mumbled.

Matt raised his eyebrows.

"Alright," she said, leaning her chin on the butt of her gun and watching some cows slip by. "I said something stupid."

He shrugged. "Then apologize."

She made a face.

"No point in dragging it out," he said, pulling a medical book from his pack. "Never go to war angry," he lilted.

She grinned. "Another phrase of your mom's?"

"Well, not word for word." Matt chuckled.

Becca looked over at Neal again, whose head was inclined toward Nick like he was listening to whatever it was that Nick was saying. She could tell that he wasn't, though, because Ruth and Nick were laughing while Neal continued to stare at the floor. She sighed again.

"Oh for Pete's sake, Becca," Matt said, looking up from his book. "No more sighing, just go apologize."

"And how am I supposed to do that? Everyone in here will hear me do it. Plus, I don't want to trouble Nick and Ruth by making them move..." Becca's voice trailed off miserably.

Matt shook his head at her and rolled his eyes. Then he pulled her gun out from under her chin, picked up her bag, and shoved them into her arms. "Just go," he said, elbowing her off the bench.

Becca shook her head and resisted, but Matt was insistent. He spread himself out so she couldn't sit back down and pushed her toward the back of the truck.

"Go," he said. "And no sighing!"

Becca made another face at him, then slowly edged her way between the benches. Stepping over others' feet, she struggled to keep her balance as the truck swayed back and forth.

"Hi," she said when she was finally in front of Neal, Nick, and Ruth.

"Hey Becca!" Ruth smiled. "What's up?"

"Could you switch spots with me for a while?" was all she said.

Nick looked curiously between Becca and Neal, who still hadn't looked up.

"Sure," Ruth said, ignoring the awkwardness. "You know I don't mind sitting next to Matt."

Becca smiled gratefully. She had figured Ruth would be all too happy to switch spots and wouldn't ask questions.

Ruth grabbed her gear and got to her feet. She and Becca shuffled around each other, then Ruth made her way to the front of the truck. Sitting down next to Neal, Becca watched Ruth plop down next to Matt happily. Just like that, Matt's book lay on his lap, forgotten.

Next to her, Neal changed his position so that he wouldn't touch Becca. Nick coughed awkwardly, then turned to Lizzy on his other side. She had been sleeping, but he slapped her arm and woke her up, clearly preferring cranky Lizzy over whatever beef Becca and Neal had.

"What do you want?" Neal asked, still averting his gaze. "You made yourself clear earlier, you don't have to expand on it."

Becca's temper flared, but she swallowed her retort. "I just came to say sorry," she said.

Neal grunted.

"I know I shouldn't have said what I did. It was insensitive and awful, and I'm sorry."

Still, Neal didn't say anything. Becca waited, hoping that he would at least look up at her. He didn't.

"Oh, come on, Neal," she whispered. "You know I don't think you're a coward."

"Oh, really?" Neal finally looked up at her. She was surprised to see tears in his eyes. She hadn't seen him cry since Finn died. "I think you really do feel that way. You just didn't want to admit it until it came bursting out."

"No, I don't feel that way. I'm sorry, and I mean it." She touched his arm, but he pulled it away.

"Becca, you don't get it. You can't just say things like that and expect everything to be okay as soon as you apologize."

"But I *am* sorry." Tears sprang to Becca's own eyes.

He shook his head. "Even if you are, I know that you meant most of what you said. Especially about the lights." He spoke barely above

160

a whisper, but for some reason these words struck Becca as if he had screamed them in her face.

She turned away. "Well yeah, I think I could really make a difference now," she muttered.

"I thought you could make a difference even before the lightning," was all Neal said.

Becca didn't know how to respond. Neal closed his eyes and crossed his arms, then leaned his head against the wall of the truck. Becca watched him for a moment, hardly registering the sounds of Nick and Lizzy arguing over something and the rest of the truck laughing at them.

Becca gazed straight ahead. She didn't know what to make of Neal. One minute he was angry enough to rip her head off, the next he sounded like a disappointed parent. She sighed. From across the truck Matt groaned.

***

Hours later, the truck went over a large bump and woke its occupants up with a jerk. Mumbling and rubbing their sore heads, everyone looked around nervously. It was sometime in the dead of night now, and the truck was moving considerably slower. The road was surrounded by trees, and the silence all around set the soldiers on edge. The truck continued to decelerate, its engine humming warmly.

Finally, they came to a stop and the clinking of gates met their ears. Becca looked at the others, who were now sitting straight and alert. They were all looking at Neal with the same question in their eyes. He shrugged his shoulders and nodded at Matt. Matt leaned over and poked his head out of the truck see where they were.

Leaning back in, Matt shook his head. The others nodded and waited. Sergeant Nelson's voice came drifting back to them, but they couldn't catch what was being said. Becca began to bounce her leg. Lizzy's stomach growled loudly, and Nick stretched his neck. Matt decided to take another look. He took a longer time pulling his head in this time.

"I think we're here," Matt said. "I've seen this drive before... I think we're at Forest Ridge."

Becca tensed up, along with the rest of the truck. "Are you sure?" she asked.

"Positive."

Glances were exchanged all around, apprehension reflecting in everyone's eyes.

"They brought us to the base closest to the front?" Lizzy asked.

Matt just looked at her gravely.

"Alright! As you were!" came a shout from in front of the truck. This was followed by a loud clink, then the truck started forward again.

Neal reached down and picked up his gun, and Becca and the others followed suit. The truck slowly passed through the gates, and they watched as the two guards closed them again and stood at attention. The trees were still thick around the road, and in the late-night darkness, they could see very little.

Everyone was tense as the truck crawled forward. Becca looked at Neal again, whose pale face was still avoiding her own. She knew he felt the same way she did, though... or at least she thought so. Anyway, if they really were at Forest Ridge, they just might get the chance they had all been waiting for.

Finally, the truck came to a stop, followed by a shout from Sergeant Nelson to hop out. They did as they were ordered, though their stiff legs protested to the quick movements, then joined the rest of the regiment in lining up in front of the two trucks. Becca stood between Lizzy and Neal.

"You will wait here," Sergeant Nelson barked, and he disappeared into the building on their left.

Becca glanced around. This base was very different from the one they had left. Instead of a large U-shape structure surrounded by thick walls and open land, they were incased by a dense forest and a seemingly random assortment of buildings.

The building that Sergeant Nelson disappeared into was small and square, distinguished by little more than a door and a few windows. Directly in front of them was a larger building, and from what Becca could tell in the dark, it was built practically. It seemed very solid, and she got the impression that the interior was one open room. On the right they could see a few paths heading off to what she assumed were more buildings hiding behind the dense groupings of trees. For the one of the main training bases, it didn't look like much, and she started to wonder how long they would actually be here.

The door to the small building on the left flew open, and Sergeant Nelson came back out with another general. They all stood at attention and watched their two commanding officers closely. Walking over, the general eyed the regiment and muttered something to Sergeant Nelson. Then he looked out into the forest and waved someone over. A tall soldier moved out of the shadows and to the general's side. After listening to him for a moment, the soldier nodded and disappeared into the large, sturdy building. Becca looked at Neal, eyebrows raised. Neal shrugged, and they both looked forward again.

Sergeant Nelson was the one to address them. "Welcome to Forest Ridge. This will be your new home. You will file into the training building here, then make your way to your temporary living quarters. Tomorrow, you will be receiving your assignments. Now, gather your gear and meet in the hall."

Becca, Neal, and the others fell into line and proceeded into the training building. After passing through the doors Becca saw she had been right; they were in a large empty space, lined with more doors. A few officers stood waiting in front of the doors, a large pile of sacks next to their feet. The entire regiment filed in and stood before the officers.

"Hey newbies," said a large, dark-skinned officer. His wide smile and happy eyes gave off a comforting feeling, and Becca found it easy to listen to him as they stood in this new and unfamiliar place. "My name is Corporal Davis. We'll be showing you your living quarters for tonight and giving each of you one of these sacks. They contain your dinner."

Small mutters flew through the group at the thought of food.

"Thought you'd be happy about that," he continued. "You'll take one, then head off to your quarters. I suggest that you try to sleep once you get there, because you won't be getting much these next few days."

The regiment nodded, mouths watering already, and slowly shuffled forward. Becca stepped closer to Neal, letting two other soldiers go in front of her.

"So, why do you think we were brought here?" she asked, hoping to get him to talk to her again. "I thought they only brought soldiers who were heading out right away to Forest Ridge."

"I thought so too, but what do I know," was all Neal said.

Becca frowned at his terse reply.

"Who cares, you guys," said Nick from Neal's right. "We're getting food and a bed. We can worry about everything else tomorrow. I just want to sink my teeth into something and get some sleep."

"Honestly, I agree with Nick," said Matt, scratching his chin distractedly. "My neck is still cramped from the ride over, it'll be nice to lie down."

Neal nodded and looked over at Becca.

She blushed under his critical gaze and shrugged. "Oh, alright, I'll wait to find out tomorrow like everyone else."

They stepped forward with the line.

Why am I the only one interested in this situation? Becca thought. *They could be finally sending us out the front. We can finally get into the action.*

She took her meal from the officers like everyone else and headed through the door on the far left. Behind it was a dark hallway that sloped downward into the earth. They walked along the slick, muddy floor carefully, not trusting their tired feet. The tunnel curved as it led them deeper underground. Eventually, the ground evened out and they were greeted with strings of buzzing light bulbs which were strung along the earthen walls. Shadows were thrown around as soldier after soldier filed past.

After five minutes of trudging, they came to a stop. Up ahead they could see a large, firm metal door. Corporal Davis stepped forward and unlocked the door, then led the way in. He flipped a switch, and lights just like those in the hallway lit up a small room full of metal beds.

"Alright, here you are," Corporal Davis said. "You'll be living here for tonight. Don't get too comfortable, though. You'll have somewhere else to rest after tomorrow. Sleep tight." With a wink he left the room, closing the steel door behind him.

"Anyone else feel like we're in a prison?" Lizzy muttered.

Nick chuckled and walked over to a bed on the far right of the room. "Honestly, I don't care," he yawned. "I'm just glad we've got beds."

The others followed him as the rest of their regiment spread out, dropping their packs and filling up the beds.

Becca picked a bed between Lizzy and Neal. Neal was already on his bed shoveling down a sandwich. Digging into his bag, he pulled out an apple and glanced up at the others. "U-shgd-eah," he managed to get out. "I-gno-ur-ungy."

"I'm sorry, are you trying to say something?" laughed Ruth from the bed on the other side of Lizzy's. "We can't understand you with all that bread in your mouth."

The others laughed, and Neal pulled the pillow out from behind him and tossed it at Ruth in response. Food seemed to put him in a better mood right away.

Ruth giggled and gently tossed the pillow back at Neal. He was right though, they were hungry. Within a few minutes they were sitting silently, scarfing down their dinner.

The whole room became quite as one by one everyone finished eating and drifted off to sleep. Someone got up and turned off the lights, engulfing the room in darkness. The moist dirt around them made the room seem darker somehow; Becca couldn't help but feel like they were sleeping in a cave.

Leaning up on her elbow, Becca reached out her hand, palm open, and lifted a bag up off the floor and let it drift back down. She could barely see it, but enjoyed the feeling of using her power nonetheless.

"Bec," came the whisper of Neal's voice. "You shouldn't."

She couldn't see him, but clearly he was watching her.

"Why not?" she whispered back, ignoring the guilty feeling that pricked at her. She knew she shouldn't egg him on again.

"You know why," was all Neal muttered. Then came the sound of him rolling over. Becca put her hand down, and with a sigh, she rolled over as well and shut her eyes. It wasn't long before she too drifted off to sleep, exhaustion happily claiming her.

Chapter Thirteen

With a buzz all the lights in the underground bunker flashed on, the blinding glare rudely rousing the troop from their sleep. Groans and grunts flooded the space, and various people threw pillows over their eyes to block the light.

"Rise and shine, newbies. It's time to get moving," came the sound of Corporal Davis's cheery voice. "You've got five minutes to be out in the hall ready to go."

With that Corporal Davis left the room, leaving the grumbling soldiers to wake up and gather their things.

"What time is it?" grumbled Nick.

"How are we supposed to know," Matt replied.

Becca sat up and glanced over at Neal. His hair was sticking up at the back of his head. Becca hid a smile and slid off of her bed. Reaching down she grabbed her pack and threw it over her shoulder. Tossing her hair up in a regulation bun, she followed Lizzy and Ruth towards the door. The boys followed, yawning.

The troop shuffled down the hall, where they met Corporal Davis, who then led the way up through the tunnel. Everyone followed silently, either too tired to think or too nervous to speak.

The walk up the tunnel seemed shorter to Becca this time, and before she knew it they were back in the gymnasium. Corporal Davis signaled to them to drop their stuff in the far corner. They did this, then filed into a sleepy formation. Moments after the last member of their regiment stepped into line, Sergeant Nelson entered the room with the general from last night and five other corporals. Everyone perked up immediately. Corporal Davis joined the lineup of superiors.

"Alright, you lot," barked the general. "You've been brought here under emergency procedures. This means you will do what you're told and you will do it fast. If you don't know how to do it, you will learn it. Now you will be divided up into new squadrons and given your new assignments. Welcome to Forest Ridge."

The general then turned and left through the main door with Sergeant Nelson. The six remaining officers waited for the general to exit before turning to the regiment. Becca took a deep breath. She could feel her heart pounding. They were about to be separated and given real assignments. *This is it.*

A corporal with piercing green eyes stepped forward and addressed them. "Okay, we have been given the lists. We will read them off, then you will join your new corporal and follow them to be debriefed. You have all been selected for your squadrons based off your training in Dune Hills. There will be no transferring, so, like the general said, learn fast."

There was some nervous shuffling and a few hushed whispers. All this sounded so serious. For a fleeting second Becca wondered if they were really ready. Then she shoved the thought away. They were ready, of course they were.

The corporal on the far left began calling off names. As they were called, the soldiers stepped forward. When the corporal was done, she said "follow me," and her group headed through one of the many doors. This happened again and again as more and more soldiers were assigned to a new team and marched off.

Becca found herself holding her breath as visions of grandeur floated in her head. She saw herself with her team at the front of the line, pushing though the Lossian ranks and freeing one of the captured Edscaftian cities. She saw herself running through a rage of bullets and debris, ignoring scratches of pain as she rushed to her team's aid. Each shot she took was a perfect mark as she leapt over stones from crumbled walls and dodged Lossian missiles.

A door slammed shut behind the next group to leave, which snapped her mind back to attention. Eagerly she awaited the call of her own name. She watched as one by one the other members of her former regiment were called and shuffled off with their new teams. The numbers dwindled, and Becca struggled to hold in her impatience.

Finally, Corporal Davis was the only officer left, and Becca, Neal, Lizzy, Nick, Matt, and Ruth were the only soldiers left. The six of them glanced at each other, then back at Davis.

"Well, then," Davis said. "That leaves you six with me. After reviewing Sergeant Nelson's notes on your practice fighting and operation results, the general decided you would be the best suited to join my crew. You will follow me, and I will debrief you. And don't worry, there's only half a chance that the A-team will chew you up before the day's end."

Corporal Davis winked and headed back out the door. The six of them looked at each other again. Neal raised his eyebrows, and Becca shrugged. They then walked over to their stuff, picked it up, and followed Corporal Davis out the door.

They went past the few other buildings in sight and into the trees. Walking in single file, they followed a foot path going deeper and deeper into the forest. Their trek through the woods was silent for twenty minutes. Finally, a small cabin came into view and they headed for it, coming to a stop just outside the door.

"Okay, you can drop your stuff right here next to the door. I'm going to go inside for a moment, then I'll fill you in," Davis said. He turned toward the door, but as he reached for the handle he looked back and scanned their faces. He smiled. "You can relax now, no need to be so tense."

The group shuffled awkwardly at his words, then he turned the handle and went inside. For a minute they stood there taking in their surroundings. The cabin was at the center of a large clearing, and stood completely alone. There were scatterings of wood piles around them and many paths leading off into the trees. Becca wondered once again what kind of training base Forest Ridge really was. Every aspect of it screamed bare minimum, giving off a strong air of impermanence.

"Some morning, huh?" Nick said, interrupting her thoughts.

"You can say that again," Lizzy replied. "As soon as they said we were all going to be separated I got chills. I was so sure we were all going to be placed on different teams."

The others murmured their agreement. Becca felt a rush of guilt. It hadn't occurred to her to be concerned about that.

"I couldn't imagine not being with all of you," Ruth said.

Matt squeezed her hand. "You would have been fine," he said. "You'd adapt, then forget any of us ever existed."

She looked skeptically back at him.

"Alright, maybe you wouldn't forget us," he said with a grin. "It sounds like they have a lot for all of us to do, though. My guess is they'll keep us so busy we won't have time to think, forcing us to adjust quickly."

"Yeah?" Nick said. "Busy with what?"

"I guess we'll find out soon," Neal said.

Becca scanned all their faces. They looked worried. "Corporal Davis said we were separated based off our fighting and operation practice," she said. "You don't think—?"

"That we're about four weeks away from being sent out to the field?" Lizzy finished.

"Yeah," Becca said.

The six of them stared at each other, a million images from their one experience at the front racing through their minds. Becca looked over at Neal, only to find him staring worriedly at her. She raised her eyebrows in a question, but his face hardened and he looked away quickly. The six of them stood in silence for a few moments more.

"I thought he said he was just going in 'real quick,'" Nick complained. "How long does he expect us to wait?"

"Until I come back out, soldier," Corporal Davis said, reappearing in the doorway.

The six of them stood at attention, and Corporal Davis walked up to Nick. "You better get used to standing and waiting, soldier," he said. "You'll be doing a lot of it in the future."

"Yes, sir," Nick mumbled.

"Good. Now, if you will all follow me. I'll explain while we walk. No, no, leave your stuff here."

The six of them exchanged looks, then followed in line behind Corporal Davis. They began walking through the forest to their unknown destination. Thick, full trees surrounded them and they fought their way through bushes and other vegetation as they struggled to keep up with Davis.

For an hour they walked on in silence, everyone wondering where they were heading. Sweat dripped down their faces, hunger began clawing at their stomachs, and their feet and legs ached annoyingly. Becca wiped the sweat off of her forehead and sighed.

If only I could make myself hover, she thought. *Then maybe my feet wouldn't hurt so much.*

They walked on for another fifteen minutes before Corporal Davis spoke up.

"Alright, newbies," he said. "I suppose I should let you know why you're here now." He turned and registered their exhausted faces, then grinned. "You lucky dogs are joining my crew for reconnaissance missions."

Instinctively, Becca looked behind her at Neal, whose eyes revealed the same shock she felt. Placement on a reconnaissance team had never even crossed her mind before. This was nothing like what she had been hoping for. How was she supposed to help end the war by keeping secrets and running in shadows? Turning forward again, she locked eyes with Lizzy, who clearly also shared her feelings.

"We have two operating teams, the A-team and the B-team, which is you. Unfortunately, you will be going through very quick training. The most recent developments of this war are pushing everything forward, so we will have a mission in just a few weeks' time. Our job is simple really: We go where they tell us to, and we come back with the information they send us to get." Corporal Davis stopped and looked at them sternly. "And there is no failing."

Becca felt a sudden dread swell in her gut as she looked into his eyes. He was dead serious, *no* failing. Davis turned around again and kept walking. She shuddered and followed suit.

"There has been a lot happening in the past few weeks that we don't understand, and the Council wants answers. We're going to get them. You can tell no one of our missions or where we are going."

"Why us?" Nick asked.

"Why? Because you all did the best in group missions, that's why," Davis answered. "You know those tests you did where you were sent in to recover an item and bring it back with your team?"

"Yeah."

"Well, what did you think all that was for?" he answered.

"But almost all of us got hit every time," Neal said.

"Yeah, well… I didn't say it was easy," Davis answered in a dull voice.

They walked on in silence for a while, with the weight of this new information sinking in. Their walk became more of a trudge, and the path they were on felt more and more like a never-ending circle. Now that Becca thought about it, they had heard very little about those sent on reconnaissance missions, and even then, reports only came from one or two soldiers, never a full team.

"Anyway, because of our limited time, we'll be getting you all started right away," Corporal Davis said. He stopped walking and faced them again. "We'll start right here."

The others halted and looked around. They were in the middle of the forest, surrounded by nothing but trees.

"Where are we?" Matt asked.

"That's part of what you'll have to figure out," Davis said. "You need to find your way back to our building without being seen. The A-team has spread out throughout the forest. Don't let them see you. If they hit you, stay where you are. One of us will lead you back when the task is done. Donahue, you're in charge. Well, good luck."

With that Corporal Davis walked off into the trees and disappeared. For a moment they all stared after him; then they all turned and looked at Neal.

Chapter Fourteen

"Well, Neal," Lizzy said. "What do we do?"

Neal looked around at the others, then at the forest surrounding them. He had no idea what to do. Why had Davis put *him* in charge?

"Does anyone remember what direction we came from?" he asked.

"No," replied Nick unhelpfully. "We turned so many times, and all these trees look the same. This is ridiculous! Shouldn't he have told us more about what to do before he set us loose?"

"Come on, Nick," Becca replied. "You heard him, we don't have time for that."

"Well, I think we can do it," Ruth said.

"Of *course* you do! You think anything is possible, Ruth!" Nick retorted.

"Hey! Don't go off on her," Matt yelled. "It's not her fault you doubt us!"

Nick opened his mouth to yell back, but Becca interrupted. "Guys, knock it off! We've got to focus. He put us out here this early in the day, which means this will probably take a while, and I don't know about you, but I don't want to be out here when it gets dark."

"She's right," Lizzy said. "We should get moving."

"You know what, Lizzy—" Nick started.

"Nick!" Neal barked. "Shut up. We've got to move, and we need to be quieter. He said the A-team is out here, and I don't think there's anything stopping them from coming at us if they hear us. When we're really out there, Sarlic's men aren't going to hold back if they hear us, and I don't think these guys will either."

The others stared at him, then nodded.

"Good," he said. "Let's get moving then."

"Which way?" Becca asked.

"I think this way," he said, pointing to their left. "Davis left just over to the right of here and I don't think he would walk in the dead wrong direction, that's too obvious. So, he probably just veered a bit. We also seem to be a bit higher up, and this way goes down. I don't remember the cabin feeling like it was on high ground, do you?"

"No," Matt said. "It almost felt like we were in some sort of hidden valley."

"I thought so too. Alright, follow me then. Stay close, and keep your mouths shut unless you see something."

He looked at them all in turn, making sure they got it. Becca smiled at him, and Neal turned and set off. He heard the footsteps of the others following after him. Without even looking, he knew Becca was the one right behind him and some part of him was glad, even though she was still on his nerves. Anyway, he wanted her close just in case she tried anything again.

The group walked on, following what they thought was a good path and keeping their eyes peeled. Unfortunately, it felt like every step they took was loud enough to tell the whole forest where they were—the ground was covered with pine needles and loose brush—and every moment they dreaded hearing the sounds of their hunters.

They went on for a half hour and saw no one. Neal was starting to get nervous. He knew that the others would get comfortable soon, and careless. That would be a perfect time for the A-team to strike. He needed to stay alert. He felt a hand on his arm and jumped. It was Becca.

He stopped and looked down at her. "What's up?" he whispered.

"Someone's close," she whispered back.

He and the others peered around, listening.

"Where?" he asked.

Becca's eyes swept the trees looked around them. Her gaze stopped somewhere to Neal's left; she focused.

"Do you think they're over there?" Neal asked.

She looked uncertain. "Maybe," she said. "I don't know."

He patted her arm and turned to the others. "Alright everyone, get low and spread out. Try to find some cover. We'll wait them out and hopefully they'll miss us. If not, I guess we'll see if we can jump them... or run."

They all nodded nervously in response and crept to larger patches of trees and grass. Neal was the last to take cover. As soon as he was certain the others were out of sight he ducked behind a large tree, shrinking into the tall grass. Seconds after he had crouched down, three figures walked through the trees straight ahead.

They were walking casually, eyes scanning the forest, guns up.

I hope those are paint guns like the ones back at Dune Hills, Neal thought.

The soldiers walked a few more paces, then stopped, heads cocked. Slowly, they all pivoted in different directions, inspecting the surrounding trees. Neal glanced around as well, and felt his heart stop as he realized he could see the top of Lizzy's head.

Please don't notice, please don't notice, he silently pleaded.

One of the soldiers stopped and nudged the others. They turned and looked too. Their gaze rested four bushes away from where the top of Lizzy's head was showing. Neal's throat constricted. Warily he poked his head up and caught Lizzy's eye, which went wide with panic at seeing him. Keeping an eye on the soldiers he signaled for her to duck lower. She did so, very, very slowly. Neal watched her disappear, one eye still on the soldiers. One of them muttered something Neal couldn't hear, then started to turn. Neal dropped back down, praying he hadn't seen him.

For a few more moments the soldiers skimmed the area, then they moved on. Neal let out a slow breath of relief, but stayed put, hoping the others would follow his lead. They did, and five silent minutes later he crept out of his hiding spot. The others immediately followed suit.

"Neal! Why did you—? That was so stupid. I thought you were done for!" Lizzy said.

"Me?! Your head was poking out of the grass like a yellow turnip! I can't believe they didn't see it!"

"I've never felt my heart pound so hard in my life!" said Ruth.

"Neal, that was really risky," said Becca. "You easily could have been seen."

"I know, I know," he said. "But I couldn't let them get Lizzy." He ran his fingers through his hair in exasperation.

"Well thankfully, they didn't see either of you," Nick said. "But shouldn't we be moving?"

"Nick's right," Matt agreed. "We don't know how many others are out there."

"Right," Neal said. "Let's go, just not in the direction they did. We don't want to run into them again."

The others all murmured their agreement and trudged on. Becca moved closer to Neal again, letting out a huge breath of air in relief. He made a face in understanding.

This felt a lot more real than any of their other practices ever had. The unfamiliarity of the forest and those looking for them made it even worse. With every step Neal was worried they would run into a member of the A-team or set off some alert. He had never felt so stressed in his life, but he wanted more than anything to get everyone out of this without being caught. If he could do that, then maybe, just maybe, when they were actually out in the field he wouldn't lose any of them.

For another hour they kept moving, but now they were all on edge. Every sound caught their attention and they would all stop and listen only to realize it was just a bird or a squirrel. Once Lizzy spotted a dark shape nearby and, thinking it was a soldier, they all ducked for cover, then laughed nervously when a deer ran past instead. As they pressed on they passed three more groups of soldiers, successfully avoiding detection. They didn't know how large the reconnaissance A-team was, though, so they didn't know how many more were out there looking for them.

"We've got to be getting closer now," Becca whispered. "We've been at this forever."

"Yeah, I don't think I can take much more of this," Nick said.

Neal looked at all of them. They looked exhausted. "Hang in there guys, I'm sure you're right. I'm sure we're close."

A branch snapped on their right and everyone froze. Another snapped on their left, and they whipped their heads that way.

Becca stiffened. "Neal," she whispered.

He looked at her. Her eyes were wide with panic.

"Oh no," he muttered.

A shout came from behind them, and they spun around to see three soldiers running full force in their direction. At the same time five more came out from the sides, and Corporal Davis was one of them. They all yelled fiercely with their guns pointed right at Neal and the others, and Neal was suddenly very aware of the fact that they had none of their own.

"Run!" he shouted.

The six of them sprinted, dodging bullets as they came flying from all directions. The cracks of gunshots rang out behind them, and out of the corner of his eye Neal saw paint splattering through the trees. He registered this fact with a moment of relief, only to be filled with more panic as another paint bullet flew very close to Nick's head.

They wove in and out of trees whose branches smacked them in the face and jumped over bushes and other underbrush which threatened to trip them up. A fallen tree came up in front of them, and they managed to jump over it just in time. As they raced forward, Neal desperately willed that none of them would get hit by their pursuers. They pushed harder and harder, with no idea where they were headed, but Neal saw they weren't gaining any distance from the other soldiers, who it seemed had an unlimited supply of ammunition. *We have to try to shake them.*

"Left!" he yelled, and the six quickly veered left.

Neal bounded over another log and caught up with Becca.

"I don't think we can outrun them!" she gasped.

"We've got to try!"

"We need a diversion or something, to gain some distance."

Neal glanced over his shoulder and saw that she was right. The A-team was getting closer every second. But what could they do? Another shot sounded, and a bullet missed Ruth by a hair. Then something caught Neal's eye; it was a large pile of chopped wood off to their right. Chopped wood meant living spaces.

"Right!" Neal shouted excitedly.

They switched directions, heading straight for the wood pile. As they ran, he noticed Becca drop back to the rear of the group.

"Becca," he panted. "What are you doing?"

"Just keep running!" she shouted back at him.

"Becca?"

The group sprinted along the edge of the woodpile as two more shots went blasting over their heads. Ruth gave a scream, but they pushed on. Becca dropped a few more steps behind. A moment later Neal heard her give a loud grunt and looked back. She was moving her hands in a quick sweeping motion, and instantly the pile of logs began to tumble behind them, blocking the path. Becca let out a triumphant grin, then sprinted past Neal with a laugh. Shouts came from the other side of the logs. Neal couldn't catch any words, but he hoped it was a good sign and not because they had seen what Becca had just done. Either way, they had just gained the time that they needed.

"Come on!" he shouted. "We can still do this!"

The others let out whoops and ran harder, panting heavily. Neal could feel a stitch in his side, but pushed on. They wove between the trees and followed the path as it curved downward. In the distance, the welcome sight of the cabin finally came into view.

"We're close!" he yelled.

The others saw it too, and they changed their course toward the building.

Just a bit further, Neal thought.

They cleared another large fallen tree, but as they did two thick logs fell down only a few yards ahead. Matt, who was in the lead, jerked to a stop and pulled Lizzy out of the way of one of the logs.

"Now!" came a shout from their left.

Neal and the others turned toward the shout to see half of the A-team rushing at them, as the other half approached from the other sides. He quickly looked around for a way out, but could see nothing. His heart dropped. Within seconds, multiple shots were fired, and Neal and the others were all marked with paint.

Nick let out a half-exasperated, half-thankful cry and flopped to the ground, exhausted. The others followed suit, wiping dirt and sweat off of their faces. Neal, however, stayed standing and turned slowly toward Corporal Davis.

"I'm sorry," Neal panted. "We didn't do it."

"Actually," Davis said, smiling broadly at the group of them, "you all did a lot better than I thought you would. You almost made it back."

"But we all died."

"Yeah, you did." Davis shrugged. "But you all died together. You stuck together, and made it this far. I think you got lucky with that wood pile collapsing, but you did good. You just need to remember that when we're out there, we'll be in enemy territory. They'll know the terrain better than we do. Which means we have to be extra careful, or they'll do to us what we did to you."

Neal nodded. He was beat, and despite what Corporal Davis said, he felt like he let everyone down.

"Okay, let's get you guys something to eat," Davis said. "Then you can meet the A-team properly, and you can ask us any questions you have. Deal?"

"Deal!" said Nick, his head popping off the ground at the sound of food.

The others sounded their agreement and got up sluggishly. Davis turned to Neal with eyebrows raised. When Neal nodded, Davis headed off to the cabin. Everyone else followed, shuffling past Neal, talking over one another. Becca stopped and turned to Neal, who hadn't moved.

"Come on," she said. "We need to get something to eat."

"Becca, we failed," he said. "How are you guys all okay with this?"

"Because it was practice, Neal. Terrifying, real feeling, but practice. Anyway, now we know more about what we're getting ourselves into."

Neal shook his head.

"He's right, you know," she said. "We made it farther than I think any of us expected to."

Neal made a face and shoved his hands into his pockets.

"Come on. We did good. Now let's go eat."

Becca walked off toward the building. Neal watched her for a minute, then followed with a sigh. He was glad Corporal Davis thought they did well, but he didn't agree. He could have done better, should have done better. How was he supposed to be able to keep his friends alive on the battlefield if he couldn't even get them through a training drill?

Neal's stomach gave a loud rumble, and he picked up the pace. Whether they did well or not, he needed food. With another sigh, he shoved away his guilt and joined the others in the cabin.

Chapter Fifteen

The group now sat eating soup with the A-team in the main room of the small cabin. There was little to the place, but they wouldn't be here long anyway, so what did it matter? The room they were in now seemed to be used for the majority of activities. There were benches set up randomly along the walls, a small table with a few chairs, and a scattering of books, papers, and boxes all over the floor. Branching off of this main room were three others; two were sleeping quarters, the other a small kitchen. The bathroom was in a small building close by.

Becca sat between Lizzy and Ruth and inhaled her soup gratefully. The boys were on the other side of the room, eating just as quickly. Everyone listened carefully as Corporal Davis introduced them to the members of the other team.

"Okay, this is Capps, Knightly, Harbor, Langhe, Mills, Base, and Grubel."

Becca looked at each of the soldiers as Davis pointed them out. She recognized Knightly,

Langhe, and Mills as the three who almost saw them in the forest. She nodded at them, and they smiled back.

"They might help with your training and studying, but you should know right away that when we go out there they will not be with us. So, don't grow too accustomed to having them around."

"Sorry, sir," said Matt. "But why won't they be with us?"

"We're breaking off into two divisions, Private Carder. The information we need requires two different operations. They'll be heading in deeper than we will, as they have more training... obviously."

The A-team chuckled at this. Becca looked at them again, noting this time how much older they looked.

Are we really ready for this? she thought again. Her throat felt slightly dry as the sounds of the blasts at the front echoed in her brain. *How much more training have these soldiers had exactly? Are we really going to be able to do this on our own?* She swallowed and pulled her attention back to the present. *Of course we're ready. They wouldn't have put us here if we weren't.*

"So, you're coming with us then?" Lizzy asked.

"That's right, Private Dowling. You really think you can make it out there on your own?"

The older soldiers chuckled again, and Becca and the others looked at one another. Becca noticed that Neal didn't meet her eyes, so she continued to watch him as Corporal Davis went on.

"After we're done eating here, they're going to show you the maps. Study them and memorize them, because they're not coming with us. Then we'll take you out to test your shooting. I'll assign you your positions once we complete that. Am I clear?"

"Yes, sir," they all said.

The six of them ate in silence for a while and listened to the older soldiers as they discussed what sounded like a strategy for moving in the field. Becca kept her eyes on Neal, who was clearly lost in thought. Hopefully, he wasn't still thinking about the forest.

Ruth leaned over and whispered to Becca. "Is he alright?"

"What?" Becca asked, taking her eyes off of Neal.

"Neal. Is he alright? He looks pretty upset, and we all know you two were fighting on the truck."

Becca blushed, and the girls all looked at Neal. Matt and Nick noticed and gave them questioning looks. Becca waved her hand in a don't-worry-about-it gesture and turned back to Ruth.

"Yeah well, he seemed fine earlier," Becca said. "I'm sure he's still just brooding over our loss in the forest. He probably thinks it's all his fault. And if he is, I just might have to slap him."

Lizzy and Ruth laughed. Becca smiled and downed her water.

After they finished eating, they went into the kitchen, where each quickly washed their own dishes and placed them in a box. Corporal Davis left the cabin while the rest made their way back to the main room and the older soldiers started shuffling through books and papers.

"Okay," the one named Harbor said. "These books and papers have the maps and plans you need. Divide them up any way you want, just make sure you memorize them." Harbor handed them each a few books and piled the rest of the loose papers into Nick's hands. "You won't be needing the other books, they're only relevant to our mission."

"And make sure to focus on the paths and areas outlined in blue, not black," said Knightly. "The black lines are also only for our mission. If you memorize those—"

"You're out of luck," Grubel finished.

"We'll be training outside if you need us," Mills said.

The six nodded, then the older soldiers left the cabin.

"Great, studying," Nick said with an eye roll. "Here, Matt, you memorize it all, then tell us the important parts." He placed all the papers on top of the books Matt was holding.

"No way," Matt said. "For once, Nick, you've got to work too."

Laughing, they all sat down, pulled some of the books and papers toward them, and began studying. When they finished with one, they passed it on to the next person. Becca pored over map after map, each displaying the details of specific areas or routes. One map designated the movement patterns of the Lossians' food supplies, the other their weapons. The next focused specifically on the hills and rivers within the active war zone, while another showed all of the battles over the past few years and the lands that had been taken or lost with each one.

After an hour, Becca was feeling overwhelmed. She had only looked at about a quarter of the books and maps and was already having a hard time remembering what was what. She glanced up at the others and saw their faces wrinkled with concentration. With a small groan, she turned back to the maps. Her eyes fell on one that detailed the Battle of Wayford. She gave a sharp gasp.

Matt looked up at her with a questioning look. "Paper cut?"

Becca shook her head and turned back to the paper, propping an elbow on the table and shielding her face with her hand.

***

"Get off of that table, young lady! That is where we eat, it is not meant for climbing on with dirty boots," snapped Mrs. Wiles.

Becca jumped off of the wooden table and bounded to the other side of the kitchen. Giggling, she ran over and grabbed one of the wooden spoons off of the counter, then took aim at one of the apples sitting on the counter ledge.

"Bang!" she shouted.

Another small hand popped up out of nowhere and knocked the apple onto the floor. Then a blond head popped up and grinned broadly at Becca, who laughed and wriggled out of Mrs. Wiles' reach.

"You two girls are more trouble than an entire barn full of nine-year olds!"

Becca dropped the spoon and ran out of the kitchen. "Come on, Lizzy," she called. "Let's go outside."

"Oh no, you don't," Mrs. Wiles' shrill voice called after them. "Becca Harraway and Lizzy Dowling, you two come back here this instant! You know you cannot go into town on your own!"

Becca and Lizzy kept running, laughing as they did.

"Girls! Young ladies!" Mrs. Wiles shouted from the door of the orphanage.

Quickly climbing over the wooden fence, Becca and Lizzy gained their freedom, then sprinted down the Willow Point Lane. Laughing all the way,

Becca grabbed Lizzy's hand and the two girls turned right and headed for town.

"Let's go see if we've got any letters," Becca said. "I'm supposed to get one from my parents today."

"Okay," Lizzy said. "But I don't think I'll have any. My aunt doesn't write much."

Becca led the way down the lane, and the two small girls wove in and out of passing adults, making their way to the post office. A large man opened the door right as the girls approached it, and the two slipped under his arms and into the building.

The small stone building was full of anxious-looking people and the buzz of the radio. Becca didn't like the looks on the faces of these people much, so she hurried past them and right up to the counter. She jumped up on one of the stools and tapped the shoulder of Arlon the postman, whose dark skin contrasted sharply with his white uniform. Becca thought it made him look fancy.

"Hi Arlon," Becca chirped.

"Hello, you two," Arlon answered, giving the two girls big smiles followed by a critical look. "Did you run away from Mrs. Wiles again?"

"Only for a little." Becca shrugged. "Have I got any letters?"

"Well, let me see," Arlon said. "This will just take a moment. Here, have these while you wait."

196

Becca and Lizzy took the candies that Arlon pulled out of his pockets. "Thanks," they chorused as he walked to the other side of the counter.

Becca looked around at all the people and wondered what they were all waiting for. They were acting nervous. One lady was clutching the hand of her son, and another was tapping her foot and staring blankly at the wall. The sounds of the radio buzzed over them all.

"Sarlic Lossi has led the Lossian Nation in the latest attack against the Edscaftian military. After struggling to maintain the crossroads of Wayford, our soldiers were forced to retreat. Lossi has now claimed Wayford in the name of the Lossian Nation. Reports of heinous war crimes have come flooding in. The Edscaftian Council is meeting tonight to discuss what they call—"

"They're in," said a tall man who was looking out the window.

The adults in the post office rushed out the door and mobbed two soldiers who had just walked out of the train station. Becca slid off of the stool and hurried over to the window. She stood on her toes to see out and watched as the soldiers handled the crowd. The people backed up, then the soldiers started passing out papers.

Becca saw the people break apart, their worried faces completely changed. Some sighed and looked up from the papers with smiles, others gasped and cried loudly. Arlon walked over to the group as well. One of the soldiers handed him a stack of the papers; Arlon shook the soldier's hand and walked back into the post office.

"Another list came in?" Becca asked, still watching the crowd of people outside.

Arlon didn't answer right away, so Becca turned around to look at him. He was gazing intently at the list.

"Yeah, Becca," he said in a strained voice. "It did."

She stepped away from the window and looked questioningly at Arlon. He was eyeing her in a funny way. She didn't like it.

"What?" she asked. "What is it?"

Lizzy came up and stared at Arlon, her eyes huge. The two looked at each other, then Lizzy gasped and turned to Becca.

"What?" Becca asked again.

"There are no letters for you today," Arlon said.

"That's okay." She shrugged. "Sometimes they're late."

Arlon sighed heavily and fumbled with the stack of papers. "Becca," he said, kneeling down next to her. "You know what this list is, right?"

Becca nodded, her eyes growing wide. Arlon quietly handed her the paper. She stared at it and her eyes locked on two names: Rebecca Harraway and Alexander Harraway.

She looked up at Arlon, her eyes filled with tears. Without a word he took the paper back and pulled her into a tight hug.

***

Becca jumped as a loud thud echoed through the room. Lizzy had tossed her book onto the finished pile and was reaching for another one. Becca blinked and looked back down at her map, staring at its inscription for a minute longer. Then she pored over every known detail of the battle. She wondered when exactly her parents had died. Had they died together when the bridge exploded? Were they part of the regiment that snuck in from the side and weakened Lossi's military long enough for the Edscaftians to call a retreat? Did they get shot down on opposite ends of the field, unable to look at the other one last time? Becca gave a quiet sniff and blinked back hot tears.

She was going to do them proud. They had died on the field, but she wouldn't. Whatever it took, she was going to end this war. Becca surreptitiously held her hand over the map and twitched her hand. The right side of the map folded itself closed. Becca nodded grimly, then moved on to a book, where more harrowing stories were doubtless waiting for her.

For the next three hours they continued to study the materials. Exhaustion crept over their necks and their eyes began to ache as they read page after page of battle information. Finally, Nick threw down the last book in his pile and flopped onto his back with a loud sigh.

"We're done. Please tell me we're done," he said.

"Yeah, alright," Neal said. "I think we can be done."

"Thank goodness," Nick sighed.

Neal reached over and dropped a heavy book on Nick's stomach. The others laughed as he folded up with a loud grunt. Then they gathered all the books and papers back together and piled them into some of the boxes. Becca stretched and looked around. Already, it felt like today had been a very long day, and the sun wasn't even setting yet.

"What are we doing now?" she asked.

"Some more training, I think. Shooting, right?" Lizzy said.

"Yeah, and the others said they were leaving to train ages ago," Ruth said. "What are they doing that's keeping them out there so long?"

"No idea," Matt said.

"Want to find out?" Nick asked. He got up and headed for the door.

The others looked at Neal, who shrugged, then led them out of the cabin.

Once outside they all took deep breaths, enjoying the fresh air. The other team was nowhere in sight. Neither was Corporal Davis, so they decided to just stretch and hang out until someone came back. Becca sat down on the ground and looked at the forest around them. It was peaceful, and nothing like Dune Hills. There, everything had been wide and open. She could stand outside and see for miles. But here, she was surrounded by a thick forest of green trees. It made her feel sheltered, protected, like the war was far away instead of just a few miles to the north.

Ruth sat down next to Becca. "It's nice, isn't it?" she said. "I love how quiet it is. It lets us hear the birds. I feel like we could never hear the birds sing back at Dune Hills."

"Yeah," Becca said. "They seem so peaceful."

"You know, I've always wished I could fly like them. I think flying would be so freeing. You could just soar through the air and feel the wind rush against your face. And if you went fast enough, the ground below would become a blur. Just a huge green blur."

Ruth was looking up, gazing at the bit of sky scattered between the branches of the trees. The small smile on her face made her look so happy, almost like she was experiencing flying right now. Then she met Becca's gaze.

"What?" she asked.

"Nothing," Becca said with a shake of her head. "It's just...You're not like the rest of us, Ruth. You always notice these things that we don't. I mean, we're all down here, and I feel like you're up there," she said, pointing at the sky. "In a good way, though," she hastened to add.

Ruth shrugged and shook her head. "No, I'm here too, Bec, but I don't know, I guess I just don't want to let this war take away all of the good things life has to offer, you know? I mean, growing up in a training camp, it really kept everything focused on fighting, and the war. My brothers really picked up on that, and they're pretty grounded like you guys... It's just, I don't want to spend all my life thinking about that. There has to be more, right? More than fighting, and kill or be killed," she said.

"I guess," Becca said with a shrug. "I've never really thought about it. It's always just..."

"Learn how to fight, do your family proud, do our Nation proud," Ruth finished.

"Well, yeah." Becca shrugged and shot her a questioning look. "You think they're wrong?"

This time Ruth shrugged. "I don't know. I just sometimes wonder why we're even fighting this war."

Becca turned toward Ruth, who was still gazing at the leaves above them. *She doesn't want to fight either?*

"We're fighting because Sarlic is trying to take over our Nation," Becca said with heat. "He already took over the northern half, and we can't let him take the rest of the Nation! You've heard what he does to the people and the villages he takes over. How many people he's killed. Imagine what he would do if he won! We have to get him. We have to get him back for everything he's done."

Ruth nodded mildly. "I know. We fight for our Nation, for our people, and for freedom... but no one ever seems to think about the being free part."

Becca blinked. "What do you mean?"

Ruth finally looked down and over at her. "Well, have you ever thought about life after the war? What you would do. What life would be like. Who would still be in it." Her gaze drifted over to Matt.

Becca didn't answer. She could honestly say that she hadn't ever thought beyond the war, but somehow admitting that to herself made her feel small. She certainly didn't want to admit it to Ruth. Ruth, who right now was probably picturing a future with Matt. A future that at this moment just wasn't possible.

Ruth sighed and looked back up at the trees. "No, I suppose you haven't. I guess I'm just weird."

"No," Becca said, shaking her head. "It's not weird, Ruth... Honestly, we'd probably be better off if more of us were like you."

Pulling her eyes back down from the forest canopy, Ruth smiled and gently squeezed Becca's hand. Then she stood up and walked over to Matt.

A free life. One without the war. One where I could choose to do anything? Where my family could still be alive?

Why had this possibility never occurred to her before? Was there something wrong with her for not thinking about it? Did the others think about it?

Becca looked across the clearing at them. Matt and Ruth were standing very close to one another, talking quietly. Were they talking about this future Ruth dreamed about? Matt said something and Ruth laughed.

Becca smiled. If anyone could have that future, she knew those two could. She let her eyes wander, and they landed on Neal. He and Lizzy were listening to Nick blab about something— probably something stupid again, because Becca could tell they were trying hard not to laugh at him.

Suddenly, she felt very alone. Her five friends had never seemed so normal as right now, and she felt anything but normal. Maybe they had thought about life without the war, but Becca couldn't see how her life could be anything *but* the war, especially now. She could feel the urge to use her power pulling at her. It had been pulling all day, and it was hard not to use it. It felt like she was shoving down a part of herself. She wanted to sneak off and practice it some more.

Power. She didn't like that term, she didn't want to call it that. New gift? Nope. That was weirder.

She wanted to see if she could lift a log, maybe two, instead of just making them tumble. She hadn't had time to really practice back at Dune Hills, and she wanted to know if she could do anything else. Besides, she had never been able to lift anything heavier than a chair. She wanted to see if she could lift something heavier now. She needed to get away to practice. The others couldn't know; Neal had made that much clear. Then again, why was she listening to Neal?

He doesn't get it. He doesn't know how it feels to be able to do this. Maybe I should just tell everyone. They wouldn't mind. Who would they tell, anyway? Then I could practice this, well, whatever this is around them.

Becca sighed. She couldn't tell them. She hated to admit it, but some part of her felt that Neal was right. She was going to have to keep this a secret. What if the news spread? What would the sergeants and generals do? What if the Lossians found out? What would they do? Would they try to get to her?

I'd like to see them try, Becca thought with a grin.

Just then, Corporal Davis walked back into the clearing. Everyone stopped talking and looked at him expectantly.

"Ah, good," he said. "You're done. You memorized everything?"

"Well, we've studied all we could, sir," Matt said. "I don't know if I can say we've memorized everything, though."

"You will study more over the next few days, then. It's very important that you remember what you read. We're going to need that information once we are out there. We will have no contact with anyone, so we must be as informed as

205

possible. Now, let's see how your shooting is, shall we?"

Becca looked at the others, who all straightened up a little. This was something they knew they were good at.

"Follow me then, let's see what you can do," Davis said. With that, he turned and headed around the cabin. The others followed right behind, but Becca stood up slowly and brought up the rear, hoping that she could shoot as well as they would today.

At the back of the cabin was a shed. Corporal Davis pulled out a key and unlocked the shed. He then pulled the handle and swung open the shed doors to reveal a large stock of weapons.

"Alright, each of you grab a gun and some paint bullets, then head back to the front of the cabin."

They did so, and again Becca was the last. She watched the others make their way around the corner of the cabin, waiting for the edge of Lizzy's boot to disappear. Once she was sure they were gone, she lifted her gun above her head and tossed it. She watched the gun for a second, and it seemed to fall in slow motion. She then stretched out her hand and the gun stopped in mid-air, floating right in front of her. Becca smiled. It felt good. She swished the gun to the right, then to the left, before pulling it back toward herself. She caught it and held it ready. She then stretched her hand out to the shed doors and watched as they closed themselves.

Trying to hide her smile, she jogged around the cabin to join everyone else.

Becca could see Neal's back disappearing into the woods on the other side of the clearing. She rushed over and caught up to him. He turned around and looked at her questioningly.

"What took you so long?" he asked.

"Oh, you know," Becca said. "Stuff." She let go of her gun and Neal looked down at her hands to see the gun hovering freely in the air. He sighed heavily.

Becca wiggled her eyebrows and gently elbowed him forward. She watched him shake his head, but he didn't turn around. She grinned to herself again; it felt good to use her power. Yeah, she would call it a power. Using it made her feel more... whole.

And if I figure out how to use it in battle, maybe I really can make a difference.

Spirits now raised, she set off after the others with a happy trot.

Soon the team found themselves in another clearing. Opposite from where they were standing were a series of targets scattered in different positions. Some were higher up, others stood alone, a few half hidden behind a tree or a large boulder, and several grouped together in the middle of the clearing. Corporal Davis turned to them.

"Alright, the testing is pretty basic," he said. "You will rotate through each of the firing positions. Every position will test a different skill, thereby showing which one will be the best for each of you when we work as a team. I'm sure you already have a good idea about which positions you work best in, but I'm testing you anyway."

The others nodded. That sounded fair.

"Okay, each target has a different range, and you'll be firing at them from different positions. For these grouped ones, I want you lying in the grass or ducking behind a boulder, up close and personal," he said, pointing behind him. "For the others, the shooting spots are also prearranged—I've marked each spot you should be at with a red stone. You'll take a shot from each position, so just pick a place to start, rotate through, and pray you don't miss because, yeah, I'm judging you."

The group chuckled.

"Alright, set up," Davis ordered.

The six of them scattered, each heading off to one of the various positions. Becca walked over to the far left of the clearing to one of the open shots. As she crossed the clearing, she passed Matt, who was setting up behind one of the boulders.

"You ready?" he asked.

"More ready than you," she said.

Matt waved her away as he loaded his gun. Becca smirked and kept going.

Corporal Davis shouted at them from the back of the clearing. "Alright, go ahead and start!"

208

Becca quickly jogged the rest of the way to her spot. Turning, she looked at the target she was supposed to hit and raised her gun. She kept it steady, took a deep breath, and tightened her finger around the trigger.

After firing she held her position for a second, as the sound of her shot echoed around the forest. Slowly, she lowered her gun and looked. She had missed. Biting her lip in disappointment, she hurried to reload her gun.

Another shot sounded and Becca looked up. Ruth had climbed to the position on the tree ledge and shot at her target. Following the aim of her barrel, Becca turned her head to look at Ruth's target. She had hit it dead in the center. Becca smiled and gave Ruth a thumbs-up.

Ruth smiled back at her, then took aim again.

Another perfect shot. Still smiling, Becca shook her head and aimed again at her own target.

Becca hit the target this time, but only just. Lowering her gun, she shifted over to the next position. The others fired as well, giving each target a few rounds, then moving on to the next. So far, the targets had only been missed a few times... most of the misses being her own. The group shuffled through, slowly hitting each of the positions. Becca glanced nervously over at Corporal Davis as he observed them, but his face was blank. Hopefully he liked what he saw. Nick took a shot and hit one of the outer circles of his target. Then Neal took his shot and, just like Ruth, hit the bull's-eye perfectly.

They continued, each slowly making their way through the rotations. Every now and then Corporal Davis would shout at them to try a position again, and they would, hoping they were doing it right.

Half an hour passed, and the sun began to set. Finally, Corporal Davis signaled for them to stop. Lowering their guns, they faced him and waited. Davis stood still for a moment, apparently thinking, then made his way over to them. Becca and Lizzy exchanged looks—one nervous, the other excited.

"Okay, you guys. Not too bad, not too bad," Davis said. "We can work with this, though you could all still use some practice. We need to be precise and hit our targets every time. When we are out there, there will be no room for mistakes. But we'll get there.

"So, for a majority of the time when we're moving, we will either be in a wedge formation or a column formation. You will spread out and go to other positions when I tell you. The way you guys are shooting, this should work fine."

The others nodded. This sounded pretty standard.

"Miller, you're sniper."

No one was surprised.

"Donahue, Harraway, I want you two on my right. Dowling, Swartz, on my left."

Neal, Becca, Lizzy, and Nick nodded.

"Carder," Davis said, now facing Matt. "You will be in center back with Miller until I send her out. Got it?"

"Yes, sir," Matt replied.

"Good," Davis said. "We'll practice moving in our formations tomorrow. Then maybe try a few different ones. Alright? Good. Follow me, then, we're heading back."

With that Corporal Davis turned and left the clearing with the team right behind him. It was getting dark, and none of them were too keen on getting left behind.

Chapter Sixteen

Neal stood up and stretched with a loud groan. He had been sitting on the cabin floor for the past half hour, just going over the day. The others had traipsed off to their assigned rooms shortly after they had returned to the cabin, and Corporal Davis had disappeared again. Neal wasn't sure where the A-team was, but he didn't mind as he had wanted some time alone before going to sleep. Anyway, there was something he knew he had to do before he could let himself sleep.

Before he did that, though, he wanted some fresh air. He made his way over to the door and pushed it open as quietly as he could. Silently, he slipped out of the cabin and walked into the clearing. Tilting his head back and closing his eyes, he took a deep breath in, filling his lungs with the chilly air. It was refreshing.

A loud grunt and a small shout of exasperation came from behind the cabin, causing Neal to jump. Curious, he glanced around, then edged along the wall. One look told him enough.

212

A fallen tree was hovering just off the ground. Standing in front of it, moving her hands in a slow turning motion, was Becca. Her forehead was gleaming with sweat and her face was wrinkled with intense concentration.

"Becca!" Neal hissed.

Startled, she whipped around and dropped the tree. It landed with a loud thud. Neal peeked behind him, making sure no one had heard it. Detecting no response, he turned back to Becca.

"What are you doing?" he asked. "I thought you went to bed."

"What does it look like," she said, wiping the sweat off her forehead. "Practicing. I needed to see if I could lift anything heavier." She gestured toward the tree. "I can, but I can't get it to spin."

Neal stepped forward and studied her face. She was clearly exhausted, but the excitement of using her powers had lit it up in a manic sort of way. The urge to yell at her again boiled up inside of him. She was crazy for practicing while the A-team was still out here, along with who knew how many other regiments; but she had made it clear that she wasn't going to listen to him.

With a heavy sigh, he gently grabbed her hand and pulled her back toward the cabin.

"You need sleep," he said. "You only recently got out of the hospital, remember?"

Becca followed and yawned loudly. "Alright," she mumbled. "But I know it's only because you don't want me to practice."

Neal didn't respond. They made their way back into the cabin, then Becca shuffled off into the girls' room with a tired wave. He watched her leave, then slumped into one of the chairs surrounding the table.

What am I supposed to do with her? She never listens.

He dropped his head onto the table and closed his eyes. He knew he shouldn't keep worrying about her, as there were plenty of other things to worry about, but he couldn't stop himself. He didn't want her to get hurt or taken away, and she didn't even seem to care. Neal lifted his head off the table and rubbed his eyes.

Well, this isn't something I'll be able to solve tonight.

Anyway, he still had a letter to write. Corporal Davis had said they weren't allowed to tell anyone what they were doing, but that didn't mean he couldn't let his family know he'd been moved to Forest Ridge. They knew what it meant; it would be enough to tell them that.

Yawning, Neal pulled a paper and pencil closer to him, then hesitated, trying to organize his thoughts. He tapped the pencil against the table, running the past few days over in his head, trying to think of a way to tell his family what was going on without worrying them. A loud thump came from

214

the girl's room and Neal jumped. The sound of Lizzy's vicious mutters floated through the open door, followed by Becca and Ruth's stifled laughs. Neal smiled, then quickly scribbled his letter.

Hey everyone,

I hope you're all doing well. Caitlin stopped by Dune Hills and gave me updates on what you've all been up to. You sound busy helping the war effort, and we appreciate it. Hopefully the crop is good this year Dad, Caitlin mentioned that Kelly has been helping with it. Has she redesigned the whole set-up already? (Only joking, Kell) Brigid, I heard you are helping Mom at the hospital now. I know you've been waiting for a while to do that, so congratulations! And Owen, I hope you're keeping things in top-notch order around the house. We can't have anyone slacking off, Little Captain. Freya, keep an eye on those pesky chickens for me, I heard an intelligence report that their new mission is to steal everyone's socks. It's up to you to keep them in order, and I know you're up to the job.

Everything is fine here. They have been training us hard, especially the last month or so. Becca is better—I'm sure Caitlin let you know she was sick—and she's up and out here with the rest of us. They transferred our camp the other day. The regiments got split up between different camps, and ours was sent to Forest Ridge. They haven't told us too much else, but I thought you'd like to know. Stay safe, we will too.

Looking up from the paper, Neal stared at the wall. He wanted to tell them more. He wanted to tell them that his troop was about to be sent out on a dangerous mission. That Becca was acting strange and he didn't know how to help her. That he had found virtually nothing about the lights that struck her, and he was worried the Council was hiding something from them. That things were beginning to move fast and for some reason he couldn't calm himself down... But he knew he couldn't mention any of it. Neal sighed and scribbled a quick goodbye. Then he folded up the letter, slouched back in the chair, and closed his eyes.

His thoughts strayed back to Becca. It was clear she was determined to use her new power even though they still didn't know anything about it, and now that they weren't at Dune Hills anymore he couldn't continue his research. Not that he had hope of finding much anyway; it seemed almost every reference to the lights had been destroyed. He hadn't found a thing on them during their studying today.

Neal stood up, placed the letter in his pocket, and stared out the window. If the Council had for whatever reason decided to wipe all information on the lights, what did that mean for Becca? What would they do if they found out she had gained her power because of them? Nothing good... He would just have to make sure they didn't find out, then.

The sounds of the A-team making their way back to the cabin interrupted his thoughts. He picked up his pencil and hurried back to the boys' room, as he didn't feel like answering any questions about why he was still up. Setting his things down next to his cot, Neal kicked off his boots, changed into his pajamas, and jumped under his blanket. As his head hit the pillow he heard the A-team come in, whispering to one another. Neal rolled over so they wouldn't be able to see his face, and a few moments later, he fell asleep.

***

The next morning, the group was up early. Corporal Davis entered their rooms with loud shouts, and members of both the A-team and the B-team leapt out of bed and were in the main room in a matter of seconds. Davis told them to grab something to eat and sit down so he could give them an update. They did this as quickly as possible and sat silently facing him with anxious faces.

"Okay," Davis said. "There was another push made at the front last night, and our men were able to regain a bit of the land that was lost. We haven't quite recovered the High Rise River, but we have moved closer."

A flurry of mutters passed between them at this news, until Corporal Davis looked at them sharply.

"This doesn't mean we get a break. No matter what happens at the front, we still need a better understanding of what is going on. We will be training even harder today, because this mission is getting more and more important, and we need to be ready."

He turned to head out the door, then stopped and faced them again. "Oh, and I should inform you that last night I was promoted to sergeant, so you probably shouldn't call me 'Corporal' anymore."

The two teams sat in shock for a moment, then stood up and congratulated him enthusiastically. He smiled embarrassedly, but they could tell he was happy about the promotion and their reaction to it.

"Alright, alright," he finally said. "Calm down, we've got work to do."

"Yes, sir!" they all said.

He smiled and shook his head at them, then headed outside. The A-team took off into forest, giving Sergeant Davis pats on the shoulder on their way out. Then he turned to Neal and the others.

"What do you say, a two-mile run as a warm-up?"

They said nothing, but their faces still looked at him happily.

"Great," Davis said. "Get to it then!"

From that moment on, they stayed busy; Sergeant Davis kept them moving all day with running, shooting practice, and drill formations. He quizzed them on the maps and information they had read, corrected them harshly if they were wrong, and drilled the right answers into their heads. They worked hard, rejuvenated by the news of Davis' promotion and motivated by the latest bit of news from the front. By the end of the day, they were working pretty well as a team and were only accidentally giving away their location half the time.

Sergeant Davis emphasized the importance of being able to move quickly and silently in their agenda. He had the older soldiers pose as Lossians over the next few days to help make their drills more real. They hid in the forest for ambushes, or charged head on with full-force attacks. Neal and the others quickly adapted to each scenario, and then adapted again when Davis changed the rules. They studied and practiced harder than they ever had before, gradually looking more and more like the team he was striving for.

At the end of the week they were given a night off and both teams gathered outside of the cabin around a large fire, exhausted but happy. The crackling of the fire was a welcome change from the sounds of running feet, shooting guns, and yelling voices, so they lounged around breathing in the crisp fall air.

"Ugh," Nick groaned, rubbing his left shoulder. "Honestly, there were so many times this week where I thought my arm was going to fall off."

"If only," Lizzy said. "Then they'd send you home and we wouldn't have to listen to the ridiculous noises you make every time you fire a shot. *Whaha!*" she shouted, imitating him.

Everyone laughed except Nick, who gave Lizzy a hard shove.

"It is nice to have a night off," Ruth said. "It feels like we haven't had one in ages."

The others murmured their agreement, then fell into silence again. The coolness of the wind brushed their backs while the warmth of the fire glowed on their faces, creating a cozy balance between cold and heat. Neal looked up at the canopy of trees above them. A few of the stars were poking through the branches and the rust-colored leaves, and he smothered a sigh. While the walls of trees around them were comforting, he missed the openness and the view of the sky from Dune Hills.

"Well, I'm up for a game of cards. You lot in?" Harbor said, turning to his team.

"You're on," Knightly replied. "I wouldn't miss a chance to kick your butt at cards any day."

The rest of the older soldiers got up and headed to the cabin.

"Any of you newbies want to join?" Mills asked over her shoulder.

The group shook their heads.

"Alright, suit yourselves," Mills replied. Then she followed the others into the cabin, where a loud card game began. For few minutes, the group sat in silence, listening to the others play.

"How long, do you think?" Lizzy asked.

"How long until what?" Matt replied.

"How long until we hear something break in there," she said. The others smiled, and a moment later the crash of a bowl against the floor met their ears. They all burst into laughter.

Still grinning, Neal lay back, let his feet warm by the fire, and stared up at the canopy again. Overall, it had been a good week. A bit painful, but good. Sergeant Davis seemed to put a lot of trust in Neal and had let him lead a few of the routines. The drills had all gone pretty well, and this encouraged Neal. There were only a few times one of them made a critical mistake, leaving someone exposed or heading right into an ambush. He was feeling a lot better about their chances than when they had first arrived here, and that anxious feeling that had been bothering him had almost completely disappeared. Maybe they *could* pull this mission off.

As the group continued to enjoy the peacefulness of the night, Neal heard rapid footsteps coming through the forest behind him. He sat up with a jolt and stared into the trees.

"What's up, Neal?" Becca asked.

"Someone's coming."

The others turned, following Neal's stare. Now they too could hear someone moving quickly through the trees. Neal focused on the branches, his arms tensing. A moment later Sergeant Davis burst into the clearing.

"Inside," he barked.

Without hesitation Neal and the others stood and followed him inside. Davis flung the cabin door open, interrupting the loud laughter of the older soldiers. They took one look at Davis, then dropped their cards and stood at attention.

Neal and the others filed into line beside them, their hearts pounding.

For a moment Sergeant Davis stood and looked at them. Neal locked eyes with him and shuddered.

"We've been called up," Davis said.

A wave of shock ran over Neal, freezing him to the spot and stopping his breath. He blinked and looked at Becca, but didn't see her. He had thought they had another week here at least, maybe two. His mind went numb, and he struggled to take in Sergeant Davis's next words.

"We're leaving in two hours, so we need to make our final preparations quickly. You will gather only the gear you need, then go around the back to grab your weapons and ammunition. When you have done that, meet here in the front of the cabin. Harbor, Donahue, you will lead the teams to the base entrance. There you will receive your final bags of supplies. I will meet up with you and we will go into separate trucks. These trucks will drive us to our drop-off points at the front.

"A-team, you are enacting Operation Echo Chamber. You are to head off to the location you'll be given at the gate. We believe this location is where Sarlic's army has moved his latest shipment of weapons. You are to find out what these weapons are, what they can do, and how dangerous they are. B-team, we will be enacting Operation Quaking Aspen. We are heading to Eastmore. It's an abandoned battleground where the Lossians have recently used some of their new technology.

We are to collect samples and return them to our engineers. We will have roughly two weeks to complete our missions. Am I clear?"

"Yes, sir," they all said in voices less confident than usual.

"Good." Sergeant Davis looked at all of them, his face unreadable. "I won't lie. Many soldiers do not return from these missions. What we are about to do is dangerous, but necessary. If we don't find out about the developments Sarlic has been making, we could lose this war. This information is vital, and no matter what happens, we bring it back."

Neal looked back at Sergeant Davis, trying to pull his mind back into focus. Sergeant Davis met his gaze and, in that moment, and a sense of pride and duty burst to life inside of Neal. With a final nod, Sergeant Davis left the cabin.

For a second they all stood there, processing the news. Then they sprang into action, as if they had all been poked sharply in the back at the same time. Neal's mind was no longer numb; now it was spinning. They were heading out into the battlefield, and from the sounds of it, very close to enemy territory. Neal headed into the boys' room, reached under his bed, and pulled out his bag. Matt and Nick did the same, their faces as determined as his. The three of them nodded at each other, stuffed their possessions into their bags, and left the room.

Back in the main room of the cabin they were joined by the girls, and together they went outside and around the back of the cabin. The older soldiers were already there. One by one grabbed the weapons and ammunition they needed from the cabinet. Neal strapped his handgun into his belt and glanced over at Becca. She looked pale. He reached out and gripped her shoulder, and she looked up into his face. Her eyes were bright, but not in the same way as when she was excited. He raised his eyebrows in a silent question, which she answered with a small grimace. He patted her arm, then the two of them reached into the cabinet and grabbed their guns. They then made their way to the front of the cabin, where the others were already waiting.

Neal walked to the front of the group to join Harbor.

"Ready?" Harbor asked him.

"Ready," Neal replied.

"Let's go, then."

Neal and Harbor reached down for the buckets of water they had placed near the fire. In two fluid motions they dumped the water on the flames, which went out with a loud hiss. As the large cloud of smoke rose, the group took off through the forest, leaving behind the cabin and the clearing they had found so peaceful just a few moments before. Neal let Harbor take the lead, as he didn't actually know the way back to the entrance of the camp. They walked along in silence, each lost in their own thoughts. On their way they passed a few other groups and recognized some faces from their old regiment. Neal and his team didn't smile or wave, and the others watched them walk by with silent understanding.

The group followed Neal and Harbor into the gymnasium. Here, there was a table holding a pile of small sacks. They all walked over and took one. Neal opened his, quickly processing the food inside and the empty canister with it. He pulled out the canister, then walked over to the sink resting behind the table and filled it up. The others followed suit, and within fifteen minutes, they were all lined up outside ready to go.

Neal put his hand in his pocket and felt the letter he had written resting there. He scanned the area, then decided on the tiny building they had seen Sergeant Nelson enter on their arrival just over a week ago. Neal moved toward the building, feeling the others' eyes on him. Opening the door, he stepped inside to a small, thankfully empty room. There was a desk set up in the far right corner, and in front of this was a small table with a box on it. Neal walked over to the small table and looked inside the box. Resting at the bottom were a few unopened letters. He quickly scanned the addresses on top, confirming that these letters were going out, then took out his own letter and dropped it in the box. With a sigh he turned, went back out, and rejoined the others.

As Neal walked back into line he caught Matt's eye, but quickly looked away. Then they waited, but not for long. A minute later the sound of heavy tires came trailing through the dark and Sergeant Davis arrived riding in one of the two trucks entering the clearing. As soon as the trucks parked Davis hopped out and approached the group again. He took them all in, then turned to the older team and handed Harbor a sealed envelope.

"A-team," he said. "I have full confidence that you can complete this mission. Good luck." He saluted them, they saluted back, and Neal felt a shiver run down his spine.

This is it.

The A-team then climbed into one of the trucks, and the B-team, along with Sergeant Davis, into the other. Once they were all seated, Davis hit the ceiling with two loud raps. The truck set off, and after sharing anxious looks with the others Neal turned his gaze out of the back of the truck and watched as they rolled down the forest path, leaving as they had arrived, in the dark cover of the night.

Chapter Seventeen

The truck slipped through the lands quickly and quietly, and no one inside slept. As the night passed, the truck made its way out of the thick forest and wove through a few nearby towns. Around two in the morning they passed over the Elder Bridge, a long stone bridge built thousands of years ago to honor the elders of their Nation. It stretched across the Great Ravine, which was so deep that many did not dare to look down. Becca closed her eyes as they crossed; she didn't feel like exacerbating her already nervous stomach. This bridge was the only one for miles and a great defense for the Edscaftian Nation. Becca just hoped she wouldn't have to cross it again for a long time. After that the lands became hilly once more, and they watched the moon slowly slip behind the rough terrain.

The team was pale and quiet all night, hardly daring to look at one another. The echoes in the distance grew closer and closer, and the team grew more fidgety. Becca began to bounce her leg, both of her hands wrapped around the gun in front of her.

At dawn they heard the first clear sounds of war. Becca looked up from the floor and shifted in her seat to look out the back of the truck. The early morning light threw harsh shadows over the bumps of the road, making their surroundings look even grimmer. She swallowed dryly. The cracks and explosions slowly grew louder. They felt the truck stop and heard the driver shout something before moving forward once again. They passed through the blockade and drove forward into the mess.

"We're here," Sergeant Davis said.

Becca tensed up, clutching her gun tightly. Her heart was pounding and she felt jittery, but ready to move. She glanced over at the others and noticed the same determined look on their faces.

The truck came to a stop, and without a word Sergeant Davis jumped out. Becca and the others followed. As their feet hit the ground, they were given only a moment to take in their surroundings before Davis took off in the direction of a large, busy tent.

They were on the edge of an abandoned city. The back area had been set up as a temporary base which housed the general's tent. Not far off was the medical tent as well, which was swarming with medics and wounded soldiers. Supply trucks were being unloaded, then reloaded with the wounded. Tanks were pushing through, aimed for the center of the city. In front of them, within the midst of crumbling stone buildings, the sounds and sights of battle greeted them. They could see distant bursts of light from the blasts and hear orders being shouted as the Edscaftian soldiers ran back and forth in a tense effort to hold their ground.

"Wait here," Sergeant Davis ordered them. "Except you, Donahue, come with me."

Neal stepped forward and followed Sergeant Davis into the busy tent. Becca watched as they disappeared into the mass of high-ranking officers.

As they watched anxiously, a booming explosion ricocheted throughout the city. Becca's eyes widened as a cloud of smoke rose from the battle. Screams followed, the sounds of a hail of gunfire not far behind. A distant building crumbled in on itself, then tumbled over, creating a haze of chaos.

"Alright," came a bark.

Becca jumped as Sergeant Davis spoke to them and Neal filed back into line. She hadn't noticed their return.

"I know it doesn't look pretty, but that's where we're headed. This is our best shot at getting through for miles. We don't have time to go around."

He took in their pale faces.

"You can do this. Our objective is to get through, not stay and hold the ground. We push and keep pushing. Got it?"

"Yes, sir," they saluted.

"Good, stay close."

With that, Sergeant Davis turned around and jogged forward. The team followed.

Becca felt her heart rate double as their feet pounded against the ground. They ran past the remainder of the temporary camp, heading straight for the battle. Davis veered to the right to avoid a street full of tanks and trucks, following the trail of running soldiers instead. They hurried down the rubble-filled streets, turning corners with their guns up and eyes ready. The floating dust caught in their throats and every noise echoed strangely off the stone buildings. The farther in they moved, the slower and more cautious Sergeant Davis became.

The sounds of the battle steadily grew louder. Another loud blast pulsated through the city and reverberated through their heads, but Sergeant Davis pushed them onward. They turned off one street and into an intersection surrounded by buildings that had been blasted apart. Edscaftian soldiers were scattered within the rubble, taking shelter from the onslaught of enemy bullets.

"Heads up!" came a shout from their left.

Becca turned in the direction of the shout, looking about wildly. Then an intense whistling sound shrieked from above. She looked up and saw a missile flying their way.

Neal grabbed the back of Becca's jacket and shoved her to the ground. The missile hit a towering pile of rubble, and large chunks of stone and metal went soaring over their heads. Becca covered her head as fragments hit the ground, skidding and splitting apart.

"Everybody up!" Sergeant Davis ordered.

His voice sounded fuzzy, distant. Becca grunted and got to her feet. She kept close to Neal as they followed Sergeant Davis forward. Already, the Edscaftian military was pushing back, and running through the newly created hole in the debris.

"Keep low and stay close," Davis said. "This will get messy."

Becca swallowed dryly and nodded, noting the grim look on his face. Neal seemed strangely calm, following on the heels of Sergeant Davis. Becca followed after him, knowing the others were close behind her. She turned and looked at Ruth, whose face was unreadable. Ruth gave Becca a nod of encouragement, and they pushed on.

Becca breathed deeply as they moved forward, fighting for oxygen in the thick air. The loud noises of battle were making her head spin, and the hurried movement was hard to follow amidst the turmoil. She wasn't sure which way they we're going or how they were going to get through, so she simply focused on keeping as close as she could to Neal and doing her best not to panic.

The team crouched low and stayed close to the walls of the buildings. Older regiments were pushing through, firing heavily at the Lossians and shoving them back down the city's streets. Shouts like "Keep it up, soldiers!" and "Give 'em everything you've got!" rang out from Becca's left, encouraging the Edscaftian troops on.

Things became a bit of a blur as they edged their way forward, but Becca did her best to follow orders. The reality of battle was a far cry from what she had been expecting, and her head was spinning. She ran forward, shot, and ducked when ordered; she had no time to think. The others kept close and moved efficiently. Davis pulled them out of the way of the majority of the thick fighting, struggling to push through the chaos.

They wove in and out of other regiments, moving in the wake of whichever one could help push their team farther forward. Davis kept them behind the line of action, allowing the other soldiers to do their work before dodging out of their way and on to the next opening in their path. As they jumped between various regiments, Becca couldn't help but feel in awe. These experienced soldiers moved as one, communicating clearly with one another and never backing down. Their faces were grim and focused, all of their energies focused on the goal of pushing the Lossians back.

The masterful teamwork not only amazed Becca but also made one thing very clear: Neal had been right. Every time she had insisted she was ready for battle and he had hesitated, he had been right. They were not ready for this. No one could be ready for this. The number of dead and wounded soldiers they passed was higher than she wished to count. The constant explosions and blasts ravaged her ears and were broken up only by shouted orders and screams of agony. It got the point where she wished she would go deaf. Still Sergeant Davis pressed them on.

"Down!" he ordered.

The team dove beneath large boulders as a hail of gunfire came their way. Becca pressed her back against the rock and pulled her gun forward, reloading it quickly. Beside her, Lizzy and Neal were doing the same. They kept their heads low, waiting. Becca's breath came in rapid gasps.

"You good?" Neal asked, glancing over at her.

She nodded.

"Just keep breathing," he said, patting her arm.

Again, Becca nodded. She looked over at Lizzy, who grimaced back at her. The sounds of the bullets lessened.

"Here's our chance!" Neal shouted.

The three of them spun around, pulling their guns above the shelter of the boulder. They fired quickly, knowing they only had a small window before the Lossians' storm of bullets raged again. Becca couldn't tell if any of her bullets were hitting their marks, and she didn't want to know. This was a lot different from hitting a target painted on a tree. Some Lossians went down, then their firing resumed. Becca, Neal, and Lizzy ducked for cover again.

"You three," Sergeant Davis yelled to them from the shelter of another boulder. "On my signal, run left!"

They waved their understanding and tensed up. Then the whistle of another missile flew over their heads. The missile hit with a resounding blast and flung debris at them. Instinctively Becca dove to the side to get out of the way. She felt the world around her erupt as they were pummeled by flying metal and stone. Rolling over and coughing, she saw a large sharp rock sitting where she had just been crouching. Nearby, Neal scrambled to his feet and hurried over to Becca. He dragged her up with him and pulled Lizzy from the ground as well, then shoved both girls in front of him.

"Go, go!" he shouted.

Becca glanced around and realized Sergeant Davis had already taken off. She had missed his signal but saw why he had given it: Another troop of Edscaftians was rushing forward, followed by the deep rumbles of a tank. Becca scrambled out of the way of the new onslaught of gunfire.

"Come on," Sergeant Davis panted. "This way!"

They wove in and out of crumbled walls, moving farther away from the heat of the battle. The sounds dimmed the farther they crept, but this only put Becca even more on edge. Sergeant Davis signaled for them to keep quiet and move into formation. Becca and Neal moved to his right, Lizzy and Nick to his left, and Ruth and Matt brought up the rear. They shuffled forward through the maze of city buildings, ears strained for the tell-tale sounds of danger nearby.

Eventually, the team came to the entrance of an abandoned building. Sergeant Davis stopped and told the group to stay there. They nodded silently and watched him disappear. Becca heaved a deep breath and slumped against the wall. She unhooked her pack and pulled out her canteen, taking a small drink of water. The water slid smoothly down her throat and eased some of the pain that breathing in the dirty air had caused. She looked around at the others, whose faces were varying degrees of unreadable and tired.

A creeping feeling climbed up her spine. She shivered, then jumped at the sound of a rock falling behind them. She stared, hoping against hope that no one was there.

Nothing happened. Becca shook her head and looked out again, struggling to throw off the fear that they were being surrounded. She put her canteen back in her pack and secured it tightly. She strained her ears for the sound of Sergeant Davis' footsteps.

What's taking him so long?

Five painful minutes later Davis returned, covered in grime and sweat.

"Okay," he said as he knelt down and began drawing in the dirt. "Most of the fight is concentrated on our right, and I can see a path through. Unfortunately, we need to be to be on the other side of the fight in order to get to Eastmore." Sergeant Davis drew a line arching around the fight. "We'll have to take the long way around, which means passing close to some of the Lossians' temporary camps. Ruth, Matt, and Neal, I want you three to go up this building to ensure we get through. Ruth, you cover us. Matt, Neal, you cover Ruth."

"Yes, sir," they answered.

Sergeant Davis turned to Becca and the others. "The rest of you will come with me. We'll snake through and make sure the other side is clear, then they will follow. Understood?"

"Yes, sir," Becca, Nick, and Lizzy said.

"Good." He stood back up. "You three go up, we'll give you time to get into position."

Neal, Ruth, and Matt took off into the building, guns up. Becca watched them disappear and felt her insides tangle up. She didn't like the idea of splitting up. Sergeant Davis turned to them again.

"We're going through as fast as we can. If we're seen, Ruth is our only cover. So, let's not put her in that position. Deal?"

"Deal," they said.

"Good." Sergeant Davis looked up at the building, gauging its distance. They had heard no signs of a struggle. So far, things seemed to be going fine.

"Alright," Davis muttered. "We wait any longer and we're dead. Come on."

Becca, Nick and Lizzy looked at one another. Then Nick shrugged and took off after

Sergeant Davis. Lizzy and Becca followed close behind. They jogged down the rest of the deserted street, then bolted around the corner of the last building and into a wide opening. Whatever buildings had been here before were long gone. The terrain in front of them was wide open, with little but crumbled bits of stone and fallen trees to hide behind. If the Lossians had any snipers perched in the surrounding buildings the way Ruth was, then Davis was right—they'd be dead.

Sergeant Davis kept them moving at a quick pace, sprinting from one boulder to another. When he turned his head to scan their sides Becca could see his face. He was tense and sweating heavily. This did nothing to soothe her nerves. She picked up the pace. They still had a long way to go before they reached good cover. She just hoped there was no one here to take them out before they made it.

No sooner had she thought this than a shot rang out behind her and a bullet bounced off the dislodged door next to her. Becca blocked the flying shards of wood and lunged out of the way.

"Let's move!" Sergeant Davis shouted.

They began zigzagging through the rubble as Davis picked up the pace. More shots were fired behind them, but Becca didn't stop to look. Bullets flew dangerously close as they sprinted breakneck for the cover of a toppled-over shack.

"Hurry!" Sergeant Davis yelled.

"What about the others?" Becca shouted as she caught up with him.

"We'll think of something!"

Another shot blasted off a stone close by. Becca winced as bits of rock flew out and cut her cheek. She desperately scanned ahead. They were almost there, just a bit further. She leapt over a large stone, then quickly dove behind another as a bullet zipped over her head. The others were close behind her, and by moving carefully, they were able to make it to the shack.

"Now what?" Lizzy gasped.

Sergeant Davis was scanning the area. Not all of the shots they heard were Lossians'. Ruth was firing rapidly from her perch in an upper window, taking down those in range. Becca's eyes roved over the open area. There was no way to tell where the enemy soldiers were hiding.

"How do we know that none of them are making their way here?" she asked.

Sergeant Davis clenched his jaw. "We don't."

Becca felt goose bumps shoot up her arms. The firing from Ruth's perch stopped, and shortly afterward the Lossians' firing became more sporadic.

"Why did she stop?" Nick asked. "Did she—"

"They're making a break for it," Sergeant Davis interrupted. "They were watching us, they'll know we made it to cover." He turned to them, lifting up his gun. "Get ready, we'll have to cover them now."

Becca, Lizzy, and Nick followed Sergeant Davis's orders with nervous glances at each other. Carefully, they positioned themselves, following the sounds of the shots to find their targets. Becca pulled her gun up and pointed it at a high window in a building on her left. She knew some bullets had been coming from that direction, but she didn't see how she was going to be able to reach that sniper from down here.

"Here they come," Davis whispered. He raised himself off his knees, crouched low, and hurried to check the area behind them, making sure their path to escape was clear. Then he came back and joined them at their perches.

Be careful, Becca thought as she watched Neal, Ruth, and Matt slide along the edge of a wall. *Please don't get hit.*

A shot rang out. Neal, Ruth, and Matt ducked, then sprinted to a low stone wall.

Lizzy aimed her gun in the direction of the shot and fired. Becca couldn't tell if she hit her mark or not. Soon after, the steady firing resumed. Sergeant Davis flung orders at them and they obeyed instantly, adjusting their aim to closer targets. Neal and the others had picked up the pace, hurrying toward the rest of the team. Becca kept one eye on them as they ran.

They'll never make it this way, she thought.

Nick, Lizzy, and Becca did their best against these invisible enemies, but despite their efforts, it seemed like the hail of gunfire got thicker instead of thinner. It didn't make any sense. Then, as Becca ducked to dodge a bullet, she understood; more Lossian soldiers had arrived. And as she shifted her position to get a better shot, a triumphant yell came from behind them. She and the others whipped around to see a group of Lossian soldiers coming around the corner. They dove for cover, then poked their guns out in defense. Unhesitating, the Lossians shot at them, faces twisted with fury.

Sergeant Davis ordered them to fire. More shots rang out, and Lossian soldiers went down. Behind them, the shouts of Neal, Ruth, and Matt approached. The blood pounded through Becca's ears as the Lossians pushed in. They were getting uncomfortably close. Davis took three successive shots, and three Lossian soldiers went down. Then he turned around and looked at the others behind him.

"Harraway," he shouted.

Becca looked at him; he was waving her over. Ducking low, she hurried over to him and knelt down behind what used to be a large table.

"They need our help. Just aim and fire," he said.

Neal, Ruth, and Matt were almost there, but the onslaught of bullets was forcing them to veer off course. As Becca watched, she noticed that Matt's left arm was hanging limply at his side, blood dripping down it. Her mind began to numb, but she forced herself to stay focused. Eyes frantically scanning the area, she searched for the source of the attacks, hoping that someone would be close enough to hit.

A flash of light reflected off some moving piece of metal to her left. Pouncing on this, she aimed her gun and took a few successive shots. As she watched, the metal flashed again, then tumbled to the ground. Becca turned her focus to the field again, and as she did her eye caught sight of a bullet heading straight for Neal. So acute was her horror, it was almost like the bullet was moving in slow motion. Without thinking she reached out her hand and forced the bullet away from Neal. It went flying in a different direction and collided into a stone wall.

A yell came from behind her. Becca whipped around to see one of the few remaining Lossian soldiers throw himself on top of Lizzy. Sergeant Davis scrambled to her aid, tackling him to the ground. At the same time, three more soldiers were rushing over. Without a moment's thought, Becca raised her gun and took aim. Nick did the same; two soldiers went down. The third jumped over their barrier and landed a heavy blow on Nick.

Nick went tumbling to the ground with a yell of pain but was able to kick the soldier's gun out of his hands. Meanwhile, Sergeant Davis had wrestled the other Lossian off Lizzy and the two were tumbling and striking each other fiercely. Becca helped Lizzy to her feet and the two backed up. Both fights were too entangled for either of them to take a shot, so instead, Lizzy bounded forward, coming to Nick's aid.

Becca turned around just as Neal, Ruth, and Matt came sprinting towards her. She reached out her hand and yanked Neal to cover. Ruth and Matt followed quickly behind. In a second they understood what was going on, and the four of them dove in to help Sergeant Davis, Nick, and Lizzy subdue the Lossian soldiers.

It was a blur of fists and feet as they tumbled with the Lossians. Becca saw a flash of metal as a knife whipped past her face. She lurched her head back and reached out a hand out to pull the arm back. But as she reached, two successive shots rang out, and the Lossian soldiers went still. Becca let go of the soldier as if his touch burned her and stumbled backward, her eyes wide.

Sergeant Davis holstered his handgun and wiped some blood from his mouth with a grunt.

"Grab your things," he croaked. "We need to move."

The team scrambled to gather their guns, then bolted after Sergeant Davis, well aware of what was behind them. They hurried down the last few blocks and out of the city. The sound of the gunfire faded behind them, but they didn't stop. Davis motioned to the edge of a nearby forest to their right, and the team directed their feet toward its welcome cover.

Again, a shot rang out behind them. Becca looked back as a troop of Lossian soldiers reached the edge of the city. They were gaining ground fast.

"Keep going!" Sergeant Davis shouted.

They sprinted on, moving faster than Becca had ever moved before. The forest was close, but so were the Lossians. An idea popped into Becca's mind. More shots rang out, but she didn't look behind her. She made sure that she was at the back of the team as they finally reached the forest. One after another the team passed beneath the trees, but as Becca slipped in, she stopped and waited. Her heart pounded madly, every inch of her screaming at her to keep running, but she forced herself to stay. The Lossians were getting close. Becca glanced over her shoulder. The rest of the team was out of view. Quickly, she threw her hands upwards and pulled. The trees yanked themselves out of the ground from the roots and toppled over in front of her, blocking the Lossians' path. Becca turned and sprinted breakneck after the others, eager to put distance between herself and the temporarily blocked Lossian soldiers. She hoped desperately that it would be enough to buy the team time to reach safety.

Sergeant Davis continued to push them as they ran, and often changed their course to throw off the trail of their pursuers. For two more hours they hurried through the woods, until finally, Matt spotted a cave and Sergeant Davis instructed them to go in and take cover. They did so, their breath coming in sharp, painful gasps.

Sergeant Davis saw them all safely inside, then said, "I'm going out to make sure the area is secure for now. Neal, you're in charge. I'll be back soon." He ducked out of the cave, then stopped and turned around. "You're doing great," he added.

They smiled weakly at him as once again he turned and left the cave.

With a loud sigh, Becca collapsed in the back of the cave and closed her eyes. The others followed suit, and they fell into silence, too tired to talk. None of them even stirred. They gazed unseeing into the cave around them listening for the return of Sergeant Davis and hoping they wouldn't hear anyone else. To their relief, luck was with them, and fifteen minutes later Davis returned to the cave.

"It seems we've lost them for now," he said as he set his things down and joined them on the floor. "We'll lay low here for a while, then we can continue on when it gets dark. This is still hot enemy territory, so we shouldn't stay here for long."

The group nodded, too tired to say anything. Sergeant Davis took out his bottle of water and took a deep drink. Putting his bottle back in his pack, he scanned the group carefully.

"Carder, we need to clean out your wound."

Matt looked down at himself in surprise. Becca leaned over and gently lifted his arm, inspecting the gunshot wound. He had lost blood, but it didn't look too bad. Ruth groaned softly as she got up and made her way over. Matt shrugged off his pack and handed it over to Ruth, who opened it and began pulling out the necessary supplies. Becca watched silently as Ruth and Sergeant Davis followed Matt's instructions and cleaned and bandaged his wound.

When they had finished, Becca looked away and gazed unseeing at the entrance of the cave. She was more than just tired; she felt numb. She couldn't process what had just happened, what they had just done. She didn't want to process it. Looking down, she realized that her hands were shaking. To stop them, she crossed her arms tightly and clenched her fists. Then she leaned her head against the wall and closed her eyes, listening to the others.

"How long until dark?" Lizzy asked.

"It shouldn't be more than an hour or two. So now would be a good time for you to eat something and rest. We'll be moving for a while. We'll have to make it to the abandoned battlegrounds before we can take a proper stop," Sergeant Davis said.

Becca heard the others rifle through their packs for some food and water. She felt a nudge on her arm. Slowly, she opened her eyes and looked at Neal, who was passing over her pack.

"You need to eat," he whispered.

"Thanks," Becca muttered.

He looked at her curiously. "Are you okay? Did you get hit?"

"No, I'm fine." She sorted through her bag and pulled out a bar to munch on. "Just tired."

Neal nodded and turned to his own pack. Becca was grateful; she didn't feel like talking right now.

They ate in silence, too worn out to say anything more. Then Sergeant Davis called Neal up to the front of the cave, where the two kept watch while the others fell asleep. Becca stared at their backs for a while, not letting herself think, but taking comfort in their vigilance. Then she closed her eyes again, and let herself feel nothing but the coolness of the wall behind her.

Chapter Eighteen

Neal sat next to Sergeant Davis in the shadow of the cave, listening to the sounds of the others sleeping. He wanted to join them, but sleep wouldn't do him any good if the Lossians found them. He glanced over at Sergeant Davis, who was staring intently to their right. He didn't look the least bit tired. Neal scratched his head distractedly and turned his gaze to their left. Nothing.

"What do we do if we do see something?" he asked Sergeant Davis.

Sergeant Davis glanced at him. "What would you do?"

He thought for a moment. "Run?"

Sergeant Davis shook his head. "No need to make it easy for them. If they don't spot you, they can't kill you. Let them pass by, then sneak out." He shrugged. "If they do spot you, then yeah, run."

Neal grunted. He wasn't sure why Davis kept picking him for these tasks. He always seemed to mess them up somehow. He glanced behind him at the others. They were out cold. His eyes lingered on Becca for a moment. She had been unusually quiet earlier... and he wouldn't put it past her to hide an injury just so she could keep going.

Sighing, he turned back to their watch. He was still worried about her. Right before they left, she had been so eager to use her power. Now there was no telling what she would do. He had a feeling she had already used it that day, and he could only hope the Lossians hadn't noticed.

The sound of a snapping branch interrupted Neal's thoughts. He stiffened and shot a look at Sergeant Davis, who held a finger to his lips. The two of them slipped farther back into the shadow of the cave and strained their eyes for any sign of movement. Neal felt his heartbeat quicken but kept his breathing even.

He scanned the forest carefully. A rustle of leaves came from their right, and his eyes shot in that direction. Another tense moment passed, then a large doe stepped into view. Neal let out a slow stream of breath and relaxed.

"Lucky," Sergeant Davis said as they both moved back to the entrance.

Nothing else was said. The two continued to keep watch as the day gradually came to an end. Neal couldn't see the sunset from the cave, but the forest canopy glowed a deep orange as the sun's light slowly faded away. Eventually, the evening slipped into dusk and darkness began to take over. Neal shifted his position and looked questioningly at Sergeant Davis, who nodded.

Neal got up and walked back into the cave. He nudged Nick's side with his boot. "Come on man, time to get moving," he said, not bothering to whisper.

Nick grumbled and looked blearily at Neal. "Time?" he asked.

Neal nodded.

Nick sat up with a grunt as Neal made his way over to Ruth. Nick reached out and slapped Lizzy's arm until she woke up. She swatted back at him and sat up crankily.

Neal shook Ruth and Matt at the same time. They opened their eyes, took one look at his face, and without a word began gathering their things. Then Neal went over to Becca. He touched her shoulder and felt a strange shock go up his arm.

"I'm up," Becca said with her eyes still closed.

Neal looked at her for a moment and wondered if she had even slept. Then, shaking out his arm slightly, he got up and gathered his own gear before bringing Sergeant Davis his.

"Alright," Sergeant Davis said, taking a good look at each of them. "Let's go."

He stepped out of the cave. Neal followed closely behind. Soft footsteps let him know the others were right behind him.

They moved quickly but carefully, fully aware that the enemy could be anywhere nearby. Neal was grateful for the darkness; it took some of the nerve off their journey. Their time in Forest Ridge paid off as well. They knew to make as little noise as possible as they dodged broken twigs and crunchy leaves.

Silent as the shadows around them, the team slipped through the forest with little disturbance. Neal kept an eye on the moon as they journeyed on, trying to gauge how much of the night they had left. For hours, they moved onward, always alert for anything that might mean danger. Finally, Sergeant Davis came to a stop and signaled the team to move behind a large gathering of trees.

"Okay," he said. "We should be close to the edge of the forest. After that, we should arrive at the abandoned battlegrounds. There, we'll be able to take cover for the rest of the night. How are you all doing?"

The group gave noncommittal nods and shrugs. Sergeant Davis nodded. "Me too. Ready then?"

"Yes, sir," they all whispered.

As they walked on Neal fell into pace with Becca, who seemed to be keeping close to him. One glance told him that she was still on edge. She was peering around nervously and flinching at every noise. He wasn't sure how to read the look on her face. He reached out and gently squeezed her shoulder. Becca looked over at him and half smiled, then looked ahead again. He had never seen her like this before.

"Donahue," Sergeant Davis whispered.

Neal moved to the front, next to the sergeant.

"I want you to scout ahead, make sure the path is clear, and find us a place to rest. I don't think they can make it much longer."

Neal looked over his shoulder at the others. They had slowed down considerably, though they were doing their best to stay alert. He nodded and took off.

Creeping from one tree to the next, Neal approached the edge of the forest. He peeked between the large branches of a pine for a better look and for a moment he stared at the abandoned village before him. Houses and barns had been blown apart and left in scattered pieces. Some still had sections standing, others were leveled and completely overgrown with vines and wild grass. There didn't seem to be a living soul in sight. Not even a cow or a bird.

Neal pulled his gun up in front of him and moved forward quietly. He hurried from the shelter of the trees to the shadow of the nearest shack. Pressing his back against the wall, he poked his head around the corner and scanned the area carefully. It was eerily quiet, and the feeling that someone else was there haunted him. Slowly, he moved around the edge of the shack and crept forward, gun up.

Nothing stirred within the ruins of the buildings, no birds or squirrels scuttled past him; even the wind seemed to have disappeared. Goosebumps prickled to life on Neal's neck and he turned around suddenly, half expecting someone to be behind him… There was no one. He took a deep breath and pushed on.

Keep calm. You need to make sure this area is secure for the others.

Neal looked through the derelict buildings one by one, while keeping an eye on the surrounding area. Still nothing. By now he had convinced himself that if someone were here, he would already be dead. Standing in the middle of the old road he put his gun down and looked back. He couldn't see the others in the trees yet. He was still alone. Looking up at the sky, he took in a deep breath and let it out, watching the mist of his breath reflect the cold light of the moon.

Then, he strapped his gun to his back and walked over to the nearest pile of stones. He knelt down and began piling the stones on top of one another, making a small mound. Once he finished with his pile, he placed his hand on top and closed his eyes, thinking of all the soldiers who had fallen today. With a jolt he realized that for the first time, he was the reason for some of those deaths. Neal took another deep breath and looked up at the stars.

"I'm sorry," he muttered, as tears slipped down his cheek. Then his thoughts turned to his family and friends, and he looked back down.

After a few moments, Neal wiped away the tears and got back to his feet. With a final scan of the area, he decided all was clear and hurried back to the forest. Sergeant Davis and the others were just arriving when he slipped back under the cover of the trees.

"All clear," he told Sergeant Davis.

"Good," Sergeant Davis replied. "We'll take cover here tonight then, and we'll all take turns keeping watch."

The team nodded and Neal stepped out of the way as Sergeant Davis took the lead. Becca moved next to Neal again, and he gazed down at her. She looked pale and exhausted, but he didn't say anything. Instead, he put his arm around her shoulders and gave her a quick squeeze. Then they moved forward after the others.

They trooped into the abandoned village and watched as Sergeant Davis picked a place for them to rest in. He would look at a building, step inside, then come back out and gaze up and down the old road. Then he would move on to the next building. Neal and the others stood waiting as he conducted his search. Matt caught Neal's eyes and pulled a face. Neal grinned back before turning his attention back to Davis. Nick gave an exasperated sigh.

"Alright," Sergeant Davis called. "This one is good."

The team shuffled forward and followed Sergeant Davis into a dilapidated house. The house had a giant hole in its side, but there was a room in the back that had gone mostly untouched, not to mention this house still had a roof.

"We'll rest here for the night. I'll take the first watch. You all eat, then get some sleep, we'll be off again at first light," Sergeant Davis said as they trooped into the back room.

Mumbles of "yes, sir" filled the room as they all placed down their gear and huddled together against the far wall. Sergeant Davis walked over to the hole in the wall and sat down. Neal opened his pack, took a long drink from his bottle, and grabbed a bar to eat. Hardly chewing, he scarfed it down, then moved his pack behind his head to make a pillow.

The others followed suit, joining him on the floor one by one. They huddled close together to conserve body heat and fell asleep in an exhausted heap.

Chapter Nineteen

The rest of the team had fallen asleep, but Becca, who was squashed in between Matt and Lizzy, was having a hard time doing so. Her mind was reeling, and she couldn't get it to slow down. In the distance she could hear the rumbles of battle. They were much fainter than what they had put up with all day, but it still seemed like the Lossians might find and attack them at any moment.

Becca tried not to wriggle too much as she struggled to sleep. She didn't want to wake the others up. It seemed like she would be lying awake all night, and she had finally given up trying when her body mercifully gave in and she drifted off into an uneasy doze. Her dreams were haunted by images of wounded and dead soldiers. More than once, she woke up in a cold sweat and fought to shake the gruesome visions out of her head.

The third time Becca woke up, Sergeant Davis was rousing Nick to take up watch shift. When she fell back asleep, she slid into a dream where she was trapped in a room which shook with one loud explosion after another, so she screamed and screamed. Her screams echoed off the walls and grew louder and louder until she thought her head was going to split.

"Becca, wake up," Ruth's voice came to her.

Becca woke with a jolt, her eyes whipping open to see Ruth's face hovering over her own.

"It's your turn."

Becca took a deep breath and slowly extricated herself from underneath Matt and Lizzy's arms.

"Are you okay?" Ruth asked as Becca dusted off her pants.

"What?" she said, looking up at Ruth. "Yeah, of course."

Ruth gave her a concerned look. "Alright. It's just, you were muttering in your sleep a bit."

"No, I'm fine, sorry."

Ruth nodded and yawned, then settled herself among the slow-breathing group. Becca made her way over to the opening in the wall and sat down in the shadows.

It was very cold; Becca could see her breath rising up in silent mists in front of her. She leaned against the mossy stone wall, eyes scanning the deserted area around them. She wondered how much farther they had to go. Would they have to pass through another active battlefield? Hopefully not.

Becca shivered and wrapped her hands around herself. The abandoned town stretched out cold and dark before her. She wondered who used to live here, and what had happed to make them flee. Why had the enemy blown their houses apart? How many had died here? The silence all around seemed to be screaming at her now, filled with battle cries. Various images from the past day floated in her head. The city's buildings being blasted apart, debris flying through the air, blood. Too much blood. The soldier who had tried to cut her today. His empty face staring into her own. A tingling, creeping feeling shot up her spine. Becca shook herself, blinking hard.

Think of something else, think of something else, she told herself, giving her eyes a hard rub. *Maybe tomorrow we won't run into anyone else. Maybe we won't have to actually shoot.*

A grunt and a shuffling sound called Becca back to the present. She froze, frantically searching the night for a sign of movement. She strained her ears to hear a sound she hoped wouldn't come. A hand touched her shoulder.

Barely containing a scream, she jumped to her feet and whipped around, gun up.

"Whoa, calm down, calm down! It's just me, Bec," Neal said, his hands raised for her to see.

She huffed in relief. "Don't *do* that! I could have shot you!"

"Sorry, I thought you heard me."

Becca shook her head and sat back down, scanning the darkness just in case. "Why are you up?"

"Couldn't sleep," Neal said, sitting down next to her.

Becca didn't say anything but found his presence comforting. Being on guard duty wasn't so unnerving with him here. They sat in silence, keeping watch over their team in this foreign, dangerous land, until eventually Becca decided to voice what was on her mind.

"It's not what I thought it would be," she said.

Neal looked at her.

"The war. I don't know what I thought the war would look like," Becca continued. "I just didn't think it would look like this. Everything just feels so... I don't know..."

"Real and terrifying," he finished.

She nodded. "I always thought Sarlic's men would look more like monsters. After everything we've heard about them. But they didn't. It... well, it was a lot harder to shoot at them than I thought it was going to be."

He studied her face, then gave her a small smile. "It's okay to feel that way, Bec," he said. "It means you're still human."

"But you guys aren't like this! Today was terrifying, and you all seemed so calm."

258

"Trust me, the rest of us were anything but calm."

She made a face. She wasn't sure she believed him.

"You were," she mumbled, staring down at her hands. "You were amazing today."

She could feel him looking at her, but she didn't meet his gaze.

"When we were in that city… what we saw…" A shudder ran over her, and she pulled her knees to her chest. "Neal, you were right. We weren't ready for this. *I* wasn't ready for this. I thought joining the war effort would be… would be easy. That doing the things we had to do today would come easy, would be simple. But this—" Becca's voice broke, and tears spilled out onto her cheeks. She looked up at him. "Neal, this was terrifying. I could barely breathe, I could barely keep myself moving, but you… you just knew what to do."

He shook his head. "No, I didn't. I just followed orders."

"No, you did more than that. No wonder Sergeant Davis picked you as his second this morning. If he doesn't make it, you'll know exactly what to do."

Shifting his position, Neal leaned against the wall behind him and faced Becca.

"No, I won't," he said, agitatedly running his fingers though his hair. "I have no idea how

Sergeant Davis does what he does, or why he even keeps picking me. I mess up every task he gives me! And I never have the right answers. At least at Forest Ridge, when I made those mistakes, we could just practice again the next day, but here..."

He looked away from her and out into the night, giving a frustrated sigh.

A small smile escaped Becca as she wiped away her tears. She wasn't surprised he couldn't see why they would follow him. Why they had been following him for weeks now.

"You're better at it then you think," she said.

Neal grunted, but didn't say anything for a while.

"Is this why you didn't sleep in the cave earlier?" he eventually asked.

"Yes," she whispered.

"Good, I was worried you were hiding an injury."

"No injury. You got close to one, though."

"What do you mean?"

She picked up her gun and pretended to examine it.

"When we were in the city, and you, Matt, and Ruth were crossing the opening. A bullet almost got you. I didn't mean to, but I just reached out my hand... and the bullet went flying the other way." She chanced a glance at Neal, whose face had gone blank. "I don't think Sergeant Davis noticed, though."

She put her gun back down and met his gaze.

"I know you don't like me using this power," she whispered with a glance at the others, who were still fast asleep on the other side of the room. "But Neal, when I use it… it feels right. Better than shooting does, anyway. I don't have to think as much, it just happens, and it works, and it—"

She stopped, worried about what Neal would say.

"It what?" he asked, his dark eyes searching her own.

"It makes me feel whole. Like some part of me I never knew was missing is suddenly back."

His face didn't change. She couldn't tell what he was thinking. Eventually he nodded and looked back out into the night, scanning the empty terrain.

"Well, thanks for saving me," he said.

Becca rested her chin on her knees, and they continued the watch together. She was grateful he didn't leave.

Turning on the spot, she checked on the others, who were still lying in a large heap. She saw that Matt and Ruth were holding hands, and a small twinge of envy twisted inside her. Her mind slipped back to the talk she had had with Ruth back in Forest Ridge. She turned forward again and chanced a glance at Neal, whose figure was silhouetted against the light of the moon.

"Do you ever think about after the war?" she asked, fiddling with her gun again.

Out of the corner of her eye, she saw him look over at her.

"Ruth does, and I don't know... I just never really thought about it much. But she said we're all so focused on fighting for our freedom that we never really stop to think about what we will do with it once we have it," she said in a rush.

It was quiet then, and Becca continued fiddling with her gun, waiting for him to say something. She kept her eyes down, and the silence stretched on. When she couldn't take it anymore, she put the gun down and looked up at Neal, ready to brush over her question, only to find him already staring at her in a way he never had before.

"Yeah," he finally whispered. "I've thought about it."

Becca's heart skipped a beat, and they continued to gaze at each other. Neal reached out and gently pushed a loose lock of hair behind her ear, his eyes never leaving hers. Becca felt her breath catch in her chest, stumbling over her pounding heart. Then she blinked and looked away, blushing furiously. She could still feel his steady gaze on her, and she was grateful for the dark.

Neither of them said anything more during the rest of the watch, but Becca felt the comfort of Neal's presence radiating off of him and filling her with warmth. They sat close to one another, neither daring to move. Eventually, Becca's shift came to an end. Neal smiled at her and told her to get some sleep, assuring her he would take the next one.

She stood up, wanting to say something to him but not really sure what. So, she just put her hand on his shoulder and said good night.

"Night, Bec," he whispered back.

She crept over to the others and settled back down on the stone floor, still feeling a warm glow in her chest. She looked over at Neal, who was once again silhouetted by the moonlight. Smiling to herself, she closed her eyes and drifted off into a less troubled sleep.

Chapter Twenty

The first light of dawn was barely edging over the horizon when Sergeant Davis woke everyone up. He ordered them to eat quickly because they would be heading off very soon, and then he went to check the perimeter. When he came back five minutes later, they all rose hurriedly to their feet and slung their packs over their shoulders. Davis told them it was time to go, and without another word he went back out of the opening. They followed him out and continued their mission, heading northeast.

The day went by much like the prior—running and crouching hour after hour, slowly making their way to Eastmore. Thankfully, they didn't run into many enemies. A few squadrons passed by, but they were able to take cover and let Sarlic's soldiers pass them without any interaction.

For four more days they journeyed on, trying hard to go undetected. This area of the front line did actually seem to be abandoned, at least for now; so they continued on, hoping that the heavy fighting would remain focused in other regions. They traversed empty flatlands as swiftly as they could, running from one broken-down truck to another to avoid being seen. They also passed through a few more towns, which thankfully had long since been deserted by their inhabitants. Sergeant Davis still ordered them to proceed with caution, so they checked buildings and kept close to the shadows.

Very few buildings were left standing in these villages, and the team couldn't help but marvel at the destruction that battle could cause. Becca's thoughts turned to Ruth as they left the last of the villages behind. Ruth ran quietly with the others, her face pale but set. If it bothered her to see towns like the one she had been driven from as a child, she wasn't showing it. Becca took strength from this, and following Ruth's lead, she pushed forward.

On day five Sergeant Davis seemed to get a little more excited.

"We're very close," he said to them as they took a quick break. "Once we arrive at Eastmore, we'll do some poking around. See what bits of machinery you can find. We're looking for stuff that seems unfamiliar and important. The A-team can tell us how these things work as a whole, but that information won't be helpful if we don't bring back some samples for our engineers to work with."

The team nodded, then Sergeant Davis stood back up and they followed suit. Quietly, they moved forward, heading for a nearby forest which stood mostly intact. With any luck, what they were looking for would be just beyond these trees.

Becca shivered as they headed into the forest, and a strange feeling scurried up her spine. Shaking her head, she told herself it was just the cold from the wind. In front of her Neal stopped suddenly, and she walked right into him.

"Sorry," she whispered, taking a step back.

"Watch your step, there's a hole right here," he said. He glanced over his shoulder at her, then paused. "Are you okay, Bec?"

Becca tried to wipe the apprehension off her face. "Yeah, I'm fine. Just tired is all." She pushed forward, gingerly stepping over the whole. "You coming?" she said over her shoulder.

Neal followed right behind and stayed close to her as they advanced. Becca was glad he did. This forest was putting her on edge, and she wasn't sure why. *Knock it off*, she told herself. *Focus, we have a job to do.*

For an hour the team continued through the trees, picking their way through thick underbrush and avoiding the loud crunch of the fallen leaves. Finally, Sergeant Davis stopped and told them to huddle up. They moved in, ready for his orders, when a deep thud echoed through the forest. Everyone froze. Shivers ran up Becca's spine again. Another thud sounded, followed by a shout. Becca felt as though a stone had dropped into her stomach. They weren't alone.

"Formation," Sergeant Davis whispered. "And stay low."

Becca and Neal moved right, Nick and Lizzy moved left, and Matt and Ruth hung back; then they moved forward as one, following Sergeant Davis closely with their eyes peeled and ears alert. Every twig that snapped or squirrel that scurried past caused them to jump, so they moved forward cautiously, guns always at the ready. A clearing was slowly coming into view and the various noises grew steadily louder. More shouts and yells were drifting over to them, followed by strange electrical buzzes and the clatter of crumbling stone. Becca looked at Lizzy, whose eyes were as wide as her own, then at Ruth, who was very white. Lastly, she stole a glance at the boys, all of whom had beads of sweat shining on their focused faces. Becca took a slow, steadying breath as they crept closer.

Sergeant Davis signaled for each of them to duck behind a tree. Becca moved to crouch behind a particularly large one, then very slowly glanced around the edge of it. She felt her jaw drop at what lay in the gully below.

Eastmore was no longer abandoned, and whatever old pieces of weaponry used to be here were long gone. The old battlefield had been cleared out and was now crawling with thousands of soldiers and dozens of large tanks. Only, some of these tanks looked nothing like what the Edscaftian military had. The large cannon on top had a purplish glowing stripe down the side and a twin glow coming from the bottom. The tanks' shape was sleek, made to fit through smaller spaces than the Edscaftian ones could. There were seven of these new tanks lined up and pointing at the last remaining ruined buildings of the city.

Off on the far side of the clearing was something large and unfamiliar: a big steel object shaped like a ship, only with no mast or sails. As they watched, two men walked into a door on its side. A few moments later a loud whirl filled the area and this ship rose to hover above the ground. Becca couldn't believe what she was seeing; a glow seemed to be coming from underneath in the colors purple, blue, and green.

Then someone down below shouted, and all seven of the glowing tanks began to hum loudly. Another shout, and seven booms erupted from the tanks simultaneously. Becca gasped as purple, green, and blue blasts fired out of the cannons and smashed the buildings opposite them into tiny pieces. Becca looked away and over at Neal, whose face registered pure shock. She knew what he was thinking—those colors were the same as the lights that had struck her. The two of them looked at Sergeant Davis, who had turned ashen.

"We need to report this back to headquarters," he whispered hoarsely. "They've got to know what's coming."

Another shout reached their ears, but this time much closer, sending a shock of panic through Becca's veins. The shout had come from behind them, through the trees. Becca turned and saw at least fifty Lossian soldiers making their way forward, guns raised.

"They've seen us!" Ruth said.

"Run!" shouted Sergeant Davis.

The team needed no prompting. The Lossians had begun firing at them, so they moved quickly to get out of range. With nowhere else to go, they headed to the right, hoping to stay under the cover of the forest. They sprinted hard as they dodged between trees, praying the bullets wouldn't hit them from behind.

Becca glanced back and saw some of the soldiers breaking off to the side, planning to block any exit. Then the pounding of more feet came from the path in front of them. They were being closed in, and would be trapped in a box of Lossian soldiers in a matter of minutes.

"We're never going to make it this way!" Becca yelled.

Sergeant Davis's head whipped in all directions as they ran. Becca saw his face harden in determination. "This way, then," he called. "This is going to be rough!"

With that he turned sharply left, heading out into the open and swarming field of Eastmore. The team followed close behind. They raced through the trees and scurried down the slope towards the heavily occupied gully. It wasn't long before the thousands of soldiers and seven tanks spotted them.

Shouts went up around them as all the Lossian forces focused on Sergeant Davis and his team. Becca didn't have time to think; she sprinted after Davis, hoping desperately that he knew what he was doing.

"This way," Davis barked, gesturing at a nearby ditch. "We can take cover behind this— Ugh!"

He fell, tumbling down the slope. Neal and Becca were right behind him, so they bent over and helped him up. Then, supporting him, the three stumbled their way to the ditch he had been pointing to. One by one the team jumped in, the bullets from behind them flying over their heads.

"Ah…" Sergeant Davis winced in pain as he pushed himself into a sitting position. Becca stared in horror as she noticed the bloodstain on his sleeve growing and his arm hanging limp beside him.

The team looked at each other, then at Sergeant Davis, panic reflecting on each of their faces. Becca turned to Neal. All color drained from his face as he stared down at the sergeant.

"What are we going to do?" Becca asked.

"We need to find a way out of here," Sergeant Davis answered, making as if to stand up. "Ah!" He pulled his wounded arm up in pain, breathing heavily.

Becca turned to Neal again just in time to see his gaze sharpen and his mouth set in resolve. He knelt down and gripped Davis's good shoulder. "What's the plan?" he asked.

"Way out," Davis grunted. "We need a way out."

Neal didn't hesitate. "Matt, bandage him up the best you can. Nick, Lizzy, cover us. Don't let the Lossians that followed us from the forest us get any closer. Becca, Ruth, see if there's a way we can get out of this ditch."

Everyone nodded and did as he said. Neal joined Lizzy and Nick at the edge of the ditch and they fired rapidly, holding back the enemy while Ruth and Becca scrambled over to the other side of the ditch. They slung their guns over their backs, scurried upward, poked their heads over the top, and scanned the area. The tanks were slowly being turned in their direction, and many of the soldiers were rushing at them. Others hung back, smirks visible on their faces. Becca and Ruth looked at each other.

"We're not going to make it out of this," Ruth muttered.

Becca didn't say anything. Still skimming the area, she noticed how the forest resumed on the other side of the clearing and extended down the far slope of the gully. If they could get past the tanks then maybe, just maybe, they could climb up and lose the Lossians in the forest. Becca nudged Ruth and pointed it out to her.

"What do you think?"

Ruth's gaze followed Becca's arm. "It's a long shot," she said. "But what choice do we have?"

The two turned and looked back in the direction Neal, Nick, and Lizzy were shooting. Despite their best efforts, the Lossian soldiers were getting closer. It wouldn't be long before they were at the ditch, and once that happened they were done for.

"Come on," Becca said.

She and Ruth scrambled back down ditch and ran over to Matt and Sergeant Davis.

"Well?" Neal asked, coming down from the other edge.

"The forest continues on the other side of the clearing," Becca answered. "If we can get over there, maybe we can shake them?"

Neal looked at her doubtfully, then down at Sergeant Davis, who was already reaching for his gun.

"Let's do it," Sergeant Davis said. "It's the best shot we've got. Swartz, Dowling, how's it looking?"

"If we're going to move, we better do it now, sir," Nick said.

"Right then, let's go."

Nick and Lizzy came down from their perch and the team headed off to the other side. They clambered up the opposite wall, giving Sergeant Davis a hand. Once up top, they were exposed again. Becca's gun was still strapped on her back, so she pulled her handgun from its holster and fired across the ditch as the others sprinted off. Once she was sure the rest of the team was out of range, she was right behind them.

They sprinted breakneck toward the forest as shots rang out behind them, hundreds of yards to go. Becca felt goose bumps prickle the back of her neck and glanced to her left. The cannons were about to fire.

"EVERYBODY DOWN!" she bellowed.

The rest of the team took one look over their shoulders and fell to the ground. A moment later jets of light blasted out of three tanks, soaring over their heads and into the forest. The blasts collided with the trees, sending bits of wood flying in every direction, some straight towards them. Becca quickly rolled to the side to dodge a large branch, then scrambled to her feet to dodge another. The others hurried to their feet as well, springing forward with the cloud of dust as cover. Catching up with Neal and Sergeant Davis, Becca looked over her shoulder once again and saw the Lossians about to fire the rest of the cannons.

"Look out!" she shouted as she grabbed Sergeant Davis by the arm and shoved him to the ground. Another blast ricocheted off a tree, its trunks and branches splintering in every direction. The team moved quickly to avoid the shower of debris as they were engulfed in a new cloud of dust. Becca hurried to her feet once more, squinted through the thick air at the way ahead, helped Sergeant Davis up, and broke into an all-out sprint.

Coughing and stumbling through the dust, Becca and the others pushed on, heading straight for other end of the gully. They wove their way between large stone fragments and jumped over fallen trees and scattered branches. There wasn't a moment to think about what they were doing; all they could do was run and search desperately for somewhere to take cover before the soldiers and tanks fired again.

A few particularly thick fallen trees appeared through the dust. Matt spotted them first and signaled to the others to follow him. They quickly changed course and made for their cover. They ducked behind the huge logs as more bullets came soaring in their direction, missing them by inches. Becca gasped for breath, a stitch stinging in her side.

"Now what?" Matt panted.

"Now we get out of here," Sergeant Davis said. "Anyone got any bright ideas?"

Becca glanced over the edge of the log and felt her stomach drop at what she saw. They were setting up missiles on top of the tanks. The tanks' cannons might need some time to recharge, but those missiles didn't.

"We need to take out those men on the tanks," Becca replied. "If they fire missiles at us, we'll never make it."

The others poked their heads over the logs to see what she was looking at. Nick let out a low groan.

"I'll do it," Ruth said as she ducked back down.

Matt started. "Ruth, no! It's too dangerous."

"I'm the best shot," Ruth said, her face calm and eyes focused. "Becca's right, we're not going to make it if they fire those missiles at us. I'll keep them at bay so you guys can move."

"Ruth," Matt said. "If they see you—"

"I'll be fine."

Matt looked at her, fear in his eyes.

"She's right," Neal said. "She's our best shot."

"You better get moving then," Nick said to Ruth. "Because they're setting those missiles up pretty fast."

Ruth nodded, then turned to Matt and pulled him into a hug. They gripped each other tightly for a moment, then she broke the hug and turned away. They all watched nervously as Ruth sprinted back into no-man's-land, heading for the gully wall which she would have to climb before dashing into the forest and making for one of the taller trees.

Poking her head back up, Becca gave Ruth some cover by firing at the nearer soldiers. Nick and Lizzy joined her, holding them at bay. Neal and Sergeant Davis looked over the log too, scanning the situation. Becca saw they were completely surrounded. Even if they did manage to get to the forest without getting shot, where were they supposed to go then? How were they going to double back around to get back to camp?

Becca turned to Neal once more, desperately hoping he would have an answer.

"Look out!" Nick shouted.

One of the missiles was ready to fire, and a second later a small blast told them it did. They jumped up, taking only a few steps before the missile landed behind them with an echoing explosion. The team soared into the air, helplessly tumbling amidst the rocks and rubble. Becca whirled dizzily in flight, then hit the ground hard, slamming onto her gun which was still strapped to her back. The wind was knocked clean out of her lungs, and her ears rang as she gasped desperately for breath.

Forcing out a cough, she struggled to sit up and shook her head, trying to see through the renewed haze of dust. Her handgun had fallen off to her left. She reached over to grab it, subconsciously noting the large dent in its side, jamming it and making it useless. Rolling onto her hands and knees she crawled over to the nearest splintered tree trunk. Lizzy and Matt joined her there, their faces covered in dirt, sweat, and blood. Lizzy was clutching her right arm, which seemed to be bent in a weird angle.

The ringing in Becca's ears faded a bit, and she heard a cry of pain. Frantically looking for Neal, she squinted around until she saw him and Nick leaning over Sergeant Davis. She crawled over and suppressed a shudder when she saw the large stick poking out of Davis's middle. Lizzy gasped beside her.

"Come on," Neal said. "We've got to move him. The Lossians will be here any second."

Becca, Matt, and Nick reached down and helped Neal move Sergeant Davis to cover. A gunshot rang out from above them, and Becca whipped her head around to see one of the soldiers on top of a tank fall. Looking back at the forest, she saw Ruth up in a tree, her gun poised to fire again. Sergeant Davis groaned, bringing her back to the task at hand. They shuffled as quickly as they could to the nearest form of shelter, then ducked for cover as the rapid sounds of the Lossians' guns reached their ears. They laid Sergeant Davis down and Matt set immediately to work.

"Neal, Becca," he said. "Hold him down."

The two of them grabbed either of Sergeant Davis' shoulders as Matt quickly pulled supplies out of his pack.

"Alright, sir, this is going to hurt," Matt said.

Sergeant Davis groaned weakly in reply.

The stick protruding from his torso was too large to leave as it was. Becca, Neal, and Matt exchanged worried looks, then Matt nodded grimly. They pushed down hard, knowing that was important for Davis to stay still. Matt gripped the blood-covered stick and broke a large part of it off. Davis let out a yell of pain as the jolt vibrated through his body, then he fainted.

"It's probably for the best," Matt muttered as he continued to work.

Another shot rang out from the forest, then another, and Becca could only assume that Ruth had saved them from two more missiles. She shot a grateful glance in Ruth's direction, then watched as Matt ripped off some of his field dressings and wrapped it around Sergeant Davis's middle.

Forcing herself to take another look, Becca poked her head over the stone ruins and assessed their situation. The tanks and remaining missiles were still pointed at them, but none of the men were moving forward. Becca wondered why this was. On her left, Lizzy let out a low groan, and Becca turned to see her leaning against Nick, clutching her broken arm again, eyes shut tight.

Neal moved close to Becca. "I don't think we're going to get out of this," he whispered. "We're going to have to carry him now, there's no way we're going to make it... Maybe Ruth should just run for it, she might make it back..."

Becca searched Neal's face, then looked at Lizzy, then at Sergeant Davis. He was right. Lizzy wouldn't be able to hold up her gun now, and how were they going to be able to carry Sergeant Davis and run without being killed? Becca began to say something, then stopped as another electric whir filled the air. Her eyes widened as in one horrible moment she understood why the Lossian soldiers hadn't moved forward and realized what was about to happen.

"Ruth!"

Becca sprang to her feet and dashed recklessly over open ground toward the tree Ruth

278

was perched in. The buzz whined louder. Becca could hear Neal, Matt, and Nick screaming behind her, but she didn't listen. Ruth heard Becca's shouts and looked down.

"Ruth, you've got to get down! They're going to shoot!" Becca was shrieking.

She saw Ruth's eyes widen in horror, and saw her shift her position to make her way back down. Then the electrical hum stopped. Ruth froze and looked up. Becca heard the tank fire, heard herself scream, and felt herself fly through the air as the light blast hit the trees. Once again, Becca was thrown to the ground and she yelled in pain as multiple branches slammed against her body. Dirt and dust swirled around her, blocking the sky and what was left of the trees from view.

Stunned by the impact, Becca's mind wove in and out of focus. The bitter taste of blood dripped into her mouth as she struggled under the branches, gasping for breath. A moment later she felt the weight of the branches being lifted off of her, then the touch of a warm hand on her shoulder. Through the swirling darkness she saw Neal's face swim into view and caught a glimpse of Matt's blurry figure sprinting past them. Becca pushed herself into a sitting position.

"Becca." Neal coughed. "Bec, are you okay?"

"Ruth," Becca croaked. "Ruth… We need to get her."

She tried to get to her feet, but fell over. Neal caught her and held her up. "We can't," he said, his voice breaking. "Becca, she's—"

Becca didn't listen. Breaking Neal's grasp she stumbled over to Matt and collapsed on her knees next to him. She felt her heart stop as she looked down at Ruth, who lay with her eyes open and limbs bent the wrong way. Tears that couldn't be stopped rolled down Becca's cheeks. Her insides did a somersault as she met Ruth's empty stare. *This can't be real.* Slowly, Becca looked up at Matt. He was staring numbly at Ruth's body, his eyes expressing an agony he would never be able to put into words.

Becca felt Neal's hand on her arm, trying to pull her up. "Come on," he croaked. "Come on, we've got to move—they're going to fire again. Becca... Matt..."

Becca looked up at Neal and saw tears on his face too, clearing paths down his dirt-covered face. As she gazed at him, she felt everything inside her go still. She blinked, then quickly wiped the tears off of her own cheeks and picked up Ruth's legs.

"We're not leaving her here," she said.

Neal tried to argue, but nothing came out. Without a word Matt placed his hands gently under Ruth's shoulders and began lifting her up. Neal grabbed her middle, and quickly they hurried Ruth's broken body over to Lizzy and Nick. They placed her down beside Sergeant Davis. Lizzy let out a cry; Nick looked too stunned to say anything.

Becca looked away from them as another wave of pain tugged at her heart, and focused her gaze on the tanks. They were recharging, and more missiles were being prepared for another round. The soldiers had moved out of range but were still close enough to keep them trapped—close enough even for Becca to see their smug smiles. They were enjoying this. This chance to show off their power, to test their new creations. This was just another game for them. Becca looked farther to the right, then the left, and saw still more of the Lossians branching off deeper into the forest. They were cutting them off. There was no way out anymore.

Then something caught her eye: the flying ship. It wasn't too far away, and it was completely abandoned at this point. A thought sparked in Becca's mind, and she knew in her gut what she had to do. She turned back to Neal, who was sitting against the log next to her, defeated.

"Neal," she said to him. "Do you see the ship over there?"

He glanced over the log. "Sure, but what difference does that make, Bec? Does that have guns pointed at us too?"

She shook her head. "No, it doesn't have any, but that's our way out."

He looked doubtful, but glanced at the ship again.

"Look," she said, her voice shaking slightly. "I'm going to hold them off, and you are all going over to the ship. Take Ruth and Sergeant Davis with you. If you can get on that ship, you can get out of here."

Neal's face blanched as he realized what she was saying. He shook his head and reached out, grabbing her arm. "No, Becca, no. They'll *kill* you. There's got to be a different way."

She put her own hand over his and stared fiercely into his eyes. "Neal, now *I'm* our best shot. If any of us are going to get out, I have to do this."

The two stared at each other, Neal's gaze softening with every second. "Please don't," he whispered.

Becca squeezed his hand, still holding his gaze. Then she gently pulled her fingers out of his and turned to the others.

"Guys," she said. "We've got a way out."

The others looked up at her, a moment of hope flickering across Nick and Lizzy's grime-covered faces. Already the whirs of the tanks were beginning to fill the air again. They had to move now.

"You've got to make it to that flying ship. You can fly it out of here. Take these two with you—Sergeant Davis might make it if you can get him to some help. Nick, Lizzy, you grab Sergeant Davis. Neal, Matt, grab Ruth."

"But how are we going to fly that thing?" Nick asked. "None of us have ever even driven a truck."

"I have," Matt croaked, looking like he wasn't even aware he was talking. "I drove some of the medics' trucks when I was training. Maybe I can figure it out."

Becca nodded. "Okay, good," was all she said. Her hands were now shaking.

The others scooped up Sergeant Davis's and Ruth's limp forms with numb quickness; Becca took a few steps away.

Mid-step, Lizzy stopped and turned to her. "What are you doing?" she said sharply.

Becca looked at her. The whirring of the tanks had gotten louder, and the Lossians had started yelling with excitement.

"I'm holding them off," she said.

"*What?* What are you talking about? Becca, you can't hold them off! There are too many of them!" Lizzy yelled.

Becca didn't reply. She moved forward, scanning the field.

"Becca, stop! Neal, you have to stop her!" Nick shouted behind her.

"No," Neal said with surprising calmness. "We stick to the plan. She knows what she's doing." His voice rose in command. "Follow the plan. It's our only way out."

"But—" Lizzy started.

"Let's move," Neal barked.

Becca looked back at them. The sight of Ruth's lifeless form solidified her resolve. She gave them what she hoped was a confident smile, locked eyes with Neal one more time, and turned and sprinted into the field.

Chapter Twenty-One

Blood pounding in her ears, Becca focused her gaze onto the nearest Lossian tank and ran towards it. She heard the shouts of the Lossian soldiers as they spotted her and smiled grimly. She had gotten their attention; now all she had to do was keep it. She stopped short, took in a deep breath, and let it out quickly. Then, raising her arms and thinking of Ruth, she shot all of her energy at the tank, shouting at the top of her voice.

To the soldiers' surprise the tank lifted off of the ground and hovered above their heads. It was heavier than anything Becca had ever lifted, and she strained under its weight, barely holding onto it. Jerking her hands in a revolving motion, she gave another loud cry and toppled the tank. The large metal beast tumbled over and landed on the one next to it with a fiery explosion.

Metal parts flew through the air, piercing the nearby Lossians. The heat from the blast came rushing at Becca. She squinted against it and forced herself forward.

Enraged now, the Lossians formed ranks and aimed everything they had at Becca. Fear rattled every fiber of her being, but she knew she couldn't stop. Two missiles came flying at her first; flinging her arms out in defense, Becca sent them off into the trees on her left. A shudder of exhilaration coursed through her. She could feel the power from the lights mingling with her blood, growing stronger with each desperate beat of her heart. This pushed her forward, and with another scream she thrust her hands out and forced another tank back, flipping it over and landing it on its top. The weight of the tank shattered its cannon, and its wheels spun uselessly in the air.

The Lossians' yells grew louder as they scrambled around their exploding weapons. They weren't smirking anymore. Their game had turned sour.

Becca used the rubble that lay between her and the Lossians to her advantage. She bobbed and wove among rocks and crumbled bits of old buildings as she dodged bullets. As she ran she lifted two large boulders into the air and flung them at the Lossian ranks. They retaliated, and explosions erupted to life around her as their return fire grew heavier.

A loud whistle filled the air, and with a shriek Becca dove for cover. The missile landed too close for comfort, shaking the ground around her and further clouding the air. Coughing and trembling, Becca shook her head, scrambled back to her feet, and pushed on. Her friends needed more time.

Two Lossian soldiers broke from the ranks and came running at Becca from the right. Becca made as though she was shoving them from five feet away and watched as their feet lifted off the ground. They tumbled through the air and landed on some of their fellow soldiers with a nasty crunch.

Becca pressed forward, deeper into the thick, grimy air. Her feet pounded steadily against the uneven ground. She was doing it—keeping the Lossians at bay, forcing their attention to stay on her. Another earsplitting blast reverberated through the air as a tank on the far right fired a shot. Becca braced herself for the blast, then felt her blood freeze as she saw it wasn't pointed at her. She watched in horror as the jet of light flew directly toward her team, who were still struggling toward the ship.

"NO!" Becca screamed, and without thinking she aimed all of her force at the light blast, trying to pull it backwards. For a moment, the blast seemed to slow, but that wasn't enough. With an almighty effort, she redirected her energy and tugged the blast farther to the right—it hit the trees, just missing the others. The force of the blast rushed at her, and she fell backwards, the heat scorching her face. She jumped back to her feet and faced the Lossians again.

Rage like nothing she had ever felt before flooded her body, and she jolted forward with a gut-wrenching scream. She scrambled over a broken wall and scanned the rubble around her. *You're not taking any more of my friends' lives today.*

She whipped her arms in shallow movements and flung stone after stone between her friends and the Lossian soldiers. The stones piled upon one another to form a wall for the others to run behind. Each boulder was harder to move than the last, and sweat poured down Becca's face as she finished the wall and turned back toward the army before her.

Exhaustion was kicking in now, but she couldn't stop. She knew she couldn't. They needed more time. Spreading her arms wide, she gasped for breath and felt the weight of the last tanks pull against her as she lifted them up into the air. She felt as though she was going to crumble under their weight, and a yell of pain escaped her as the pressure mounted. The Lossians' shouts doubled as they scrambled away from the tanks, and they fired everything they had at Becca.

Bullets and blasts landed all around her, sending dirt and debris in every direction, and the dust became so thick she could hardly see. Arms shaking violently, Becca squinted behind her and caught a glimpse of the others. They were almost at the ship. With a massive heave, she pulled the tanks higher. Screaming under the strain of their weight she drew her arms in, then shoved them outward, throwing the tanks backwards.

Panting and trembling violently, Becca dove to the left to dodge an oncoming missile. Her bruised body fell with a thud as the missile landed, only just missing her and leaving a deep crater in the earth next to her. Ears ringing again, she pushed herself up with a grunt and ducked out of the way of the flying bullets. The shouts around her grew louder and the onslaught grew stronger as the soldiers struggled to get near her. Becca panted as she fought off the missiles and bullets. Her arms moved defensively as she whipped the bullets and missiles one way, then another, then sent them flying back. Bits of broken trees and stone flew all around her, many cutting and bruising her. But she didn't stop.

"Ah!"

Becca let out a shout of pain as a bullet grazed her left arm. She staggered, then frantically scanned the ground around her until her eyes landed on a large scrap of metal. She pulled it in front of her and hid behind it, panting as she glanced desperately around. She didn't know what else she could do.

A new, loud hum sounded behind her and flooded her with relief. The others had made it to the ship.

Becca tried to look back at it, but the haze in the air hid it from view. She prayed they could figure out how to use it, and fast. The Lossians had heard the hum as well, and shouts of frantic orders carried over to Becca. She glanced around her small shield and saw them turning their missiles toward the ship. Meanwhile, the rest of the soldiers were still sending down a rain of bullets on Becca. She didn't know how much longer she could hold out.

More loud whistles screeched through the air as two more missiles fired, heading straight for the exposed ship. With a grunt and a gasp of pain

Becca forced herself up again, bounding out from the shelter of her shield as she aimed the last of her strength at the missiles.

She focused her mind and energy completely on the missiles, ignoring the numbing pain radiating off of her wounded arm, and pulled with everything she had. She felt the missiles slow down, but their energy was pulling against her own. Screaming with the effort it took to hold them, tears of pain streaming down her face, Becca pulled and took a staggered step backward.

She could feel every muscle in her arms screaming at her, begging her to stop. A bullet hit her right leg, and with a loud cry of pain she fell to her knees. The thick dust clogged her breath and blinded her eyes. The missiles slipped and moved forward, but she didn't let go.

She kept her focus on the ship as slowly, very slowly, the ship was gaining altitude. She didn't know what the Lossians were doing anymore. The pain from her two wounds was blinding her. Gasping for breath and trembling from the effort it took to hold the missiles, Becca watched as the ship gained enough height to get out of range of the bullets.

Come on... Get out of here, come on!

The soldiers redoubled their effort against Becca, using everything they had to stop her, to force her to let the missiles go. She heard their superiors yelling orders and knew they would be moving in. She lunged behind the metal cover once more, keeping her focus only on the missiles.

290

Fighting the urge to let go, to give into exhaustion, she held on. The ship's cold grey form hovered over Eastmore for a moment, then with agonizing slowness edged its way over the trees, and finally, mercifully out of range. Becca let out an exhausted cry and relinquished her hold on the missiles. They spun through the air and crashed into each other with tremendous force, the explosion drowning out all else.

Becca lay there, numb and drained, as she listened to the sounds of the Lossians yelling and firing at the ship. She tried to move, to sit up, but didn't even have the strength to lift her hand. Finally, the firing stopped as the ship edged its way out of sight. The piece of metal in front of Becca fell over, leaving her exposed, but she didn't move, she couldn't move. Instead, she lay still on the ground, waiting.

Two large boots emerged from the dust and swam into Becca's view. She heard angry voices but couldn't register what they were saying. Then she felt rough hands grab her and force her up onto her knees. One of Lossian soldiers punched her in the gut, and she crumpled up in agony. Another kicked her, a gun was slammed into her back, and their shouts and slurs reverberated in her head. Then a loud shout silenced the infuriated Lossians, and she felt someone reach down and tie her wrists together.

Let them take me, Becca managed to think. *It doesn't matter... not anymore...*

She was pulled to her knees again and found herself face to face with a particularly nasty-looking soldier. His eyes glinted dangerously as he looked her up and down, taking in her dirt- and blood-smeared form.

"Stand her up," he growled.

They forced Becca to her feet. She could feel her right leg shaking violently beneath her and she took in short, painful breaths, refusing to collapse in front of these men.

"You'll be coming with us," the angry soldier hissed, his face uncomfortably close to her own. Then he grabbed the hair on the back of her head and pulled.

Becca let out a small scream of pain.

The soldier smiled. Then he snatched her wounded arm and squeezed. She let out another cry, then he pushed her back to the ground.

The soldier leered down at her, his lips curling savagely around his teeth. She tried not to shudder. Then, with an angry look, he nodded to the other soldiers behind her. They each grabbed her by an arm and lifted her off of the ground. Then they carried her toward one of the few trucks still standing.

The sight of the destruction around her swam in and out of Becca's vision as they moved. Smoke and dust still clouded the air. Turning her head, she struggled to see over to the trees she and her team had hid behind. She felt Lossian soldiers drop her, then pick her up again and toss her into the back of a truck. She landed with a hard thud on the cold metal floor, but she hardly felt it. They slammed the door shut and she was engulfed in darkness.

They're safe, she thought. *They're going to make it home.*

Another thud told her that the front door had closed, and then the engine roared loudly beneath her. She closed her eyes and let out a broken sob as the truck's wheels began to turn. Inside, she felt nothing and the only thought she let herself think was that her friends were safe. They had gotten away. The rumble of the truck drowned out the yelling of the remaining Lossian soldiers who shouted insults at her through the solid metal walls. More tears slid down her face as she thought of Neal and the others. The pain became overwhelming, and Becca gave into it, sobbing quietly as the truck drove away from the smoldering remains of Eastmore and headed north into the lands of the Lossian Nation.